RIDER

L∆NNING'S LE∆P BOOK 6

KATHI S. BARTON

This is a work of fiction. Names, characters, places, and incidents are products of the author's imagination or are used fictitiously and are not to be construed as real. Any resemblance to actual events, locations, organizations, or persons, living or dead, is entirely coincidental.

World Castle Publishing, LLC
Pensacola, Florida
Copyright © Kathi S. Barton 2016
Paperback ISBN: 9781629895437
eBook ISBN: 9781629895444
First Edition World Castle Publishing, LLC, September 19, 2016
http://www.worldcastlepublishing.com

Cover: Karen Fuller
Editor: Maxine Bringenberg

PROLOGUE

"Once you have put the magic in the safe, I wish for you to come to me. And no messing around either. I have things to do." Allister nodded, but said nothing. He knew the woman to be mad as a hatter, and he did not wish to anger her again. She had a tendency to kill what made her mad, no matter how much she might need them later. "You screw this up for me, Allister, and I swear to you I will rain a bloodbath on you that you'll feel for decades. Once all the Lannings are dead, then you will be paid for what you've done here."

He had no idea how that would work. If she killed him, which was what she had implied, then there would be *no* feeling for decades. Not to mention she'd never get the safe to open if she did kill him, bloodily or not. He smiled to himself when he thought of that little clause he'd put on it.

"As you wish, my lady." He moved slowly, but his body wasn't nearly as old and frail as he let her think it was. The less she knew of him, the better. Sadly, she knew too much as it was. Sonya, a hard taskmaster on her best days, had not been happy when he'd told her that his only child had died. "Once the safe is open the magic will go to the one that deserves it, just as you have ordered."

"Yes, when the Lannings are no more and I am queen, the person who opens the door here will be my right hand man. We will rule the kingdom as one. I'm sick to death of those upstarts. From the beginning they were trouble to me. Imagine, not wanting to help me take over the kingdom. We all know that I would make a better queen than Kendra. Her being picked over me is just not right." Allister nodded again. "And when you come to me, I will expect you to bring me her head, do you hear me? I wish for proof of what you have said to me."

"There is no head, my lady. As I have told you, my child was burned at the stake some days ago. Her death, it has taken a great deal out of me. But there is no body left to bring you even a small portion of it." Sonya looked as if she didn't believe him, so Allister changed the subject. "The monies that you told me to make for you, they're all from different time periods. There are instructions on what can be spent and what cannot. The person who opens this, they will be warned. I hope you realize that should they spend the money that is there before the dates it was in use, there will be hell to pay. You know this, I'm sure."

"Never you mind about what I know or not." He knew she had no idea. The woman could barely think her way out of any trouble, much less know the way cash would work in the future. He did, but he wasn't going to tell her that. "As I have said to you, I have all the power in the world, both worlds. When this is completed, and the Lannings are all dead and cold in their graves, I will rule both worlds."

"As you wish, my lady." She eyed him hard. "I wish only for you to get what you deserve. And as surely as I am standing here, I'm sure that you will."

"Thank you." Allister watched her carefully. "When you've finished, come to me. I will be at my home. Then we will discuss what happened to your daughter. I'm glad that she's dead, if you want to know the truth of it. Her being alive, it was going to mess up my carefully laid plans. And that has happened enough of late."

Allister knew just what part his daughter had played in Sonya's game. It was why he'd taken care that the woman never touched his only child. But right now, he wanted nothing more than for Sonya to go away and leave him to his task. It didn't differ much from the one that she had set upon him, but he hoped for a better outcome. The money had come from the future. Allister hadn't manufactured it as he'd told her, but had gone to the twenty-first century and had traded some of his furniture and other items that fetched him a grand price for the cash. The future was so different than the time he now lived in that Allister had been tempted to stay there and never to return here. But there were things afoot, things that he had to see to the end so that his daughter could live. And live she would.

Graham was his child, and even though he'd told the upstart that she was dead, she was as alive as him. Hidden away so that no one, not one person, could harm her the way he knew Sonya would. Allister had sent her away, far away into the future so that she'd be safe from this monster here. He'd also taken it upon himself to make sure that no matter what, the Lannings would live. At least he hoped that he had.

When the last of the magic had been put in the large safe that he'd brought from the future with him, he closed it up and leaned heavily upon it. It was time, past time really, for him to finish what he needed to do for all mankind. Especially those that were of the magical nature such as him. Going to the mirror, he spoke to the woman that he knew would someday open the safe with a man he'd never met in person. Nildale, the king of the genjar, would help a great deal, this he was sure of. He summoned the woman there and smiled when her face appeared for him.

"I shall be dead soon. Much sooner than I had hoped. But I have left you something. It's there in the safe for you to use should you...you will need it. There is a man that will come to you. He will offer you so much, but ask for nothing in return. Take his knowledge. You will need it. You are the soul of my magic. And when you are able to understand all, you will also understand the reasons behind the things that have been set in motion for you." He thought of the woman he'd met briefly while there making the arrangements that would save so many. She was going to be stronger than any he'd ever encountered. And she'd keep his child safe. "Laci Lanning, you are going to save a great many people. And Nildale, the king, he will help you understand."

Going back to his bed after putting a spell on the mirror to keep it safe as well, he closed his eyes. Allister hurt in more places than he'd thought there were names for; the lifting and toting were hard on an old man like him. Reaching for his child, their connection so strong that there was no need for his mirror, he smiled when she appeared before him as a shadow of herself.

"You do know that I know nothing of this world. And that there are things that go fast here that scare me, Father." He nodded and smiled bigger. "She has been there then? This monster you are saving me from?"

"Yes. She has come and gone. You will be safe where you are. Do not go to the Lannings until you feel the safe has been opened. They will need your knowledge of magic and a bit more." She nodded and looked away. The pain of their parting hurt him even more than he could say. "Graham, you will be safe for me?"

"Yes. I will be. So will you." He said that he would be gone soon enough. "Nay, Father, you will not. I have decided that you will come to me."

And just like that, he stood in the little house that he'd purchased for his child to keep her safe. Sitting down, he looked at his daughter and wondered, not for the first time, how she'd become so strong.

"She will find you with me here." Graham simply told him she would not. "Yes, she will. Her magic is powerful, or so she says. You must return me to my time so that she does not find us together and destroy all that I have set up for you."

"Sonya will not only not find you, but she will fail at her attempts to follow you here. Her mind does not work as ours does. It is full of her own self, and she will think you have done something to yourself and will almost forget you by tomorrow." Allister didn't think so. Sonya wasn't strong, no, but she was evil. "I will protect you, Father. Trust me."

"I do." After he was shown to his room, a room that would only be found if he allowed it, he laid down on the big bed. There were many luxuries here, more than he'd imagined when he first arrived. When he was alone again, he thought of the precautions that he'd made for his child, and wondered briefly if him being there now would make a difference.

The Lannings were.... He willed himself to their home, a shadow of himself, so that he could watch them. He had no doubt that they'd survive this time of strife, but who he feared for most was the man called Rider.

Allister knew that the man was a good one. A bit of a worrier, but that was all right too. Allister knew that his own child would be tempered by this man, his level head and strong will would keep her safe. He watched the man now with his family, and hoped with all that he was that he'd be a good match for his only child. And that he'd keep her safe from the one that wished her dead. As surely as he stood there watching, knowing that Sonya was now dead in the time that Rider lived in, he also knew that the monster that lurked in the darkness would come for his child.

CHAPTER 1

The shop was filled with the finest things they could find. The shelves were full of linens. Small pieces of pottery and frames, and each piece of furniture was polished and ready. Laci looked around the room that she was in once more just to make sure that nothing was out of place.

"You do know that as soon as the first person comes in the door, they're going to touch something and leave a mark on it, don't you?" Laci grinned at Andrew. "I see. You think that's going to be good too."

"Yes. Maybe if they see how much work we've put into being here then they'll help me out by buying something." He just shook his head. "When you open in the morning, will you care if someone puts one of your glass door knobs in the wrong slot?"

"I won't, but Rider might. I knew that he was slightly OCD, but lately I think he's gotten worse than Max. And he's right up there with having things organized to the point that you want to murder him." Laci said she knew that as well. "I guess you would. Is he going to make it back here in time for the opening?

11

Or is he staying away too?"

"No. He said that he'd be here. I guess Max is cutting his lessons a little short so that he can be here too. I'm guessing that we'll have some time on our hands so that he can get some studying done while he's here." The bell over the door sounded and she smiled at Max. "There is the man of the hour now. How's it going?"

"I'm not sure. They're giving me a hard time about my residency." He looked so down that she wanted to go to the hospital and zap them. "But I do have some good news. David Hudson said that I could come to the clinic and work it out. He is working on getting things set up for me now."

"Wonderful news." He nodded and stowed his backpack under the front counter. "What do you think? Are we ready for the morning?"

"I think it looks better than I thought it would." As he moved around the open setting, Laci looked around as well and found herself nervous as hell. Max sat at one of the many table and chair sets they'd set up to sell. "I went to the bank this morning like you asked me to and signed all the cards. The checks look good too. They had them ready, so I brought them with me."

When Andrew joined him at the table, Laci sat on one of the rockers that they'd found. She'd set the show room up so that it looked like different rooms as one might find in a house, but with about a dozen tables and chair sets, as well as that many desks and end tables. Even the kitchen area, her favorite, looked like something from the twenties and thirties. Some things even older than that.

"Before I forget, I talked to Kendra on the way here. She said that she'd managed to find the name of the man in the mirror. His name was Allister. No last name, but that's not unusual. The safe, as you know, is from this time frame, as well as the money inside, but the man disappeared right after Sina left office all those years ago." Laci felt a little stirring over her skin and knew that it was her magic. That was his name; she knew it as soon as Max said it. "Also, there is no record as to what happened to him. Sonya was involved in the safe, as we found out, but she was never able to end their relationship. That's what the notes in her book said; he'd disappeared and their relationship wasn't completed."

"You think that she meant to kill him when he was done with whatever he did to the safe?" Max said that it looked that way. "And did we ever figure out how the safe got there, or the money inside either? I mean, there wasn't any paper money then, and some of the dates on it are just this year. Do you suppose that he was able to time travel?"

"It's not impossible." That scared her, and she decided that she didn't want to know if that was something she could now do. "Laci, you can—"

"No, don't say it. I'm still dealing with what happened yesterday." Max grinned and nodded his head. "You think that was funny? Well, I don't. That scared the living shit out of me."

"I could tell. And you didn't harm anyone with what you did. And you have to admit, from what I heard, the look on Rider's face was priceless." He had been pissed. And might well still be. "You never caused him harm, Laci, and it was only a mistake, not done with purpose."

"Yeah, well that made it no less scary for me." She did grin then. "He was sort of bent out of shape about it, wasn't he?"

She'd been putting together a bed in the showroom when she'd had a sudden thought. Rider. Nothing more than that. But almost as soon as his name popped in her head, she knew that he was in distress. Willing him to her, she screamed when he came

13

not just as his big cat, but in mid leap as well.

He'd tackled her to the floor, his big body slamming hers into the wall behind her as well as breaking two of her chairs. Rider was not amused to be caught unaware as he'd been, and even more pissed off when she commanded him to shift to check out his wounds, which left him naked and fuming in her shop.

And the reason for the stress wasn't anything that bad, really. He'd been frustrated with the lot of them, mostly his brothers, for not getting things settled before screwing around. They'd been just as frustrated, it seemed, but he wanted them to burn it off after they were done for the day. It had ended when she'd taken him away from them.

Laci looked around rather than think of how badly they'd both been frightened by what she'd done, and how he'd been pissed off that she'd made him shift to naked to see if he was all right. She wondered if he was still not speaking to her.

I'm not mad at you. His voice echoed in her mind and she smiled at him. *However, if you ever have the need to see if I'm all right or not, a simple question might save me some embarrassment.*

I'm so sorry about that. He told her not to worry about it. *How's the hunt going? Have you been able to find the bedroom furniture that you were looking for?*

That and more. I'm having the best time here. Who knew there would be this much going on down a highway meant for moving cars? She could hear his laughter. *Even Mom and Sina are having a grand time. I'm glad that you let us take the cargo van. I've nearly filled it twice over already. And my home is going to look like your showroom, only with less clutter.*

They were traveling the Historic National Road Yard Sale Days. It was along Route Forty and covered five states. She'd read about it after she'd made the date for their grand opening here or she might have gone as well. As it was, Rider was finding them all sorts of things for both her shop and the hardware store next to her that the men ran. She envied him having the time of his life.

She told Andrew and Max what Rider was saying. Max asked him if he'd been able to find any old pottery. After that, she knew that the two of them were talking and moved to the counter to see about the cash register, then to the back room where the safe had been moved.

Laci only had to run her fingers over the front of it to open it up. The big doors would open silently and then close the same way. She'd discovered quite by accident that if she walked away from it for any amount of time, it would lock itself and keep the contents safe. She looked at Andrew when he came in the room with her.

"Have you taken an inventory today?" She told him she had this morning. "And is money still showing up? And the jewelry?"

"Yes. This morning there was over five grand in there, as well as a leather bag of diamonds that I swear are perfect cuts. I'm getting sort of worried about what might show up after yesterday." He nodded and pulled her into his arms. "Do you suppose that the dagger that came has something to do with the one that was in it when I first opened it?"

"They look alike enough to have been forged by the same hand. The only difference is the jewels." Instead of emeralds and rubies, the one yesterday had been covered in amethysts, as well as diamonds. "I wonder what sort of person would have wanted something like that. And Nildale said that there was powerful magic on them. He said that he remembered the man who had made them, that he'd long since died. They're very old, older than anything we have in here, and priceless too. I've asked him to return them to his kingdom. I guess that was where they were stolen from in the first place."

"I'd like to talk to that man again. But the mirror is quiet. I had planned to ask him about them, but without knowing how to summon him, I just have to wait until he comes back." Laci glanced over at the mirror that had been hanging for weeks now where she'd first seen it. "I wish I could see her too. The woman there."

That had surprised her to no end. Seeing a woman, a beautiful woman, standing in a living room talking on a cell phone. And when she turned and saw her, presumably in a mirror of her own, she'd walked to it and it had gone dark. Like she'd turned it over or something.

"You still think she's related to the man?" She told him that she did. Laci was sure of it. There could not be two people in the world with the same color eyes like his had been. The brilliant purple could have only come from him. "I hope we get some answers soon. In the meantime, I have to get back to work. I just came over to see if you've made plans for the dinner tonight."

She'd almost forgotten about the dinner. The entire Lanning family, and there were a lot of them, were going to be at their house for a celebration. She was nervous about it, hoping that it wasn't going to jinx things, but the party was to kick off the new ventures that they were all in on. Bits and Pieces, the hardware store, as well as Lanning's Antiques and Tisket Tasket, Charlie's basket company, were set to open in the morning.

"I didn't, but Wentworth has it under control." The cook made her laugh every time she spoke to him. He was so prim and proper. "He said that he will have dinner ready at six, and that we had better not be late again. He said that he will be most displeased with us."

"Well, we can't have that. Do you know what he's fixing?" She said that she hadn't asked him. "Still afraid of him, are you?"

"A little. But he's growing on me. And I'm not really afraid of him so much as I'm in awe of him. Did you know that he's been around for more than a thousand years as a cook? The things that he's made boggle the mind."

"Yes. He told me that he's growing some of the things that he had on his planet for us as well. If he makes that chicken dish for me every night, I'll be a very contented cat." Laci didn't tell him it wasn't really chicken, but some animal from the other realm. There were some things better left untold, she thought. "Anyway. I'm heading back now. I'll see you tonight."

After a long, wonderfully warming kiss, she found herself in the office alone. The safe seemed to beckon to her, so she touched her fingers to it and waited. It didn't take it long to sing to her again.

It wasn't singing, she supposed, so much as humming. One day a few weeks ago she'd touched it and had the most overwhelming urge to go down the street to the garage sale at the corner. There she'd found a treasure trunk of items for the store. And after the second time it had happened, she had started taking the truck with her. The safe seemed to know where the best deals were.

But today it was telling her to go to the mirror. So, making her way to the lobby of the shop, she moved to the mirror. Max joined her there. He asked her what was going on.

Before she could answer him, however, the man appeared. He looked so different that she almost didn't recognize him, but for the eyes…those beautiful eyes.

"Hello, Laci, Max. How are you this fine day?"

CHAPTER 2

Graham held her breath and counted to ten. It hadn't done her much good in the past, but she was determined not to lose her temper today. Never very good at holding her tongue, today she decided that she'd do it or die. Or kill someone. Which was looking more and more like it was going to be the end result anyway.

"Are you listening to me?" Nodding, she let out her breath slowly so as not to piss off the woman in front of her anymore. "I don't think you are. If you were listening to me, I'd not have to come in here all the time and straighten you out. I have told you over and over that Howie is doing the best he can, and you should cut him some fucking slack."

"First of all, watch your language. This is a school. And secondly, he is not doing the best he can. If he was then I'm sure that his grades would reflect it." Graham stretched her neck and heard it pop. She was sure that Howie's mom heard it as well. "He's being given the grades that he earned. I'm not changing them for anyone."

"You're going to regret this. Do you have any idea how hard it will be for him to get into college if he doesn't pass this class? Hard, let me tell you. The other teachers saw it my way." Graham pointed out that she wasn't the other teachers. "No, you're not. They understand that he's going to be great someday, and you're stuck with making him learn crap that happened long before he was born. What do you think he's going to need that shit for when he's out there making touchdowns with the pros? Nothing, I tell you. Not one damned thing. Now you're going to get out that little book of yours and change that grade to one that has him passing with flying colors, or so help me, I'm going to make you regret it."

"I'm not going to change it. And our time is up." When Graham stood up, Milly Winston grabbed the arms of the chair she'd been abusing with her weight since she'd sat down. "Do you think I'm going to pick you up and throw you out? Sorry to disappoint you, but I don't think that's going to happen. I'd very much like for you to leave, please. This meeting is over."

Graham could pick her up and toss her across the parking lot if she wanted. Easily. But she doubted that throwing this piece of shit out of her room would earn her any brownie points. Instead, she went to the door and invited the next family in. As they made their way to a different part of the room to speak, Milly stood up and started shouting about how they weren't nearly finished yet. Ignoring her as best she could, Graham smiled at the nervous couple in front of her.

"Callie is doing very well in my class. I would like her to spend a little more time in writing out her answers. Sometimes it takes me a bit to figure out her code." Her mother looked at Milly then her before saying that stupid text messaging was causing it. "Yes, I can see that. But the letter U does not replace the word, as

20

well as R and a few others that she uses. If we can get her to work on that, I'm sure that she'll excel in her other classes as — "

"You aren't going to shove me under the chair, Miss Teacher." It was on the tip of her tongue to tell Milly that there wasn't a chair big enough for her to shove her under, but only continued talking to the O'Neils. "If you think you can just pretend I'm not here, then you're sadly mistaken. I'm not going anywhere until you do as you should have. He's going places, not like you have. Everyone knows that when you can't cut it in the world, you become a teacher. Is this some kinda power trip for you? Well, honey, I'm more powerful on my worst days than you'll ever be."

"I've no doubt that you think so. But as for changing grades, I'm just fine with what I gave him in the first place, thank you." She looked at the couple again. "I'm so sorry about this. But if you'd like to go to one of the other offices with me, I think we can finish — "

The body flying at her made Graham forget where she was. Putting out her hand, she just managed to shove the O'Neils out of the way with her magic before Milly hit her with her body. Even that didn't save them from being hurt, she knew, but at least they weren't smashed like she was.

Graham tried her best to get the woman off her, but before she could do more than just adjust her, the fist hit her right in the face. After a few more punches, all of them centered at her nose and mouth, Graham had had enough. Slamming her own fist into the fat face over her, she let a little of her magic go and knocked the woman off her and onto the floor. Graham stood up and went to the O'Neils, ushering them out of the room before Milly woke. Christ, Graham thought, who knew teaching should come with hazard pay?

By the time the police arrived, Milly was up screaming that

21

she was suing her. Milly claimed that Graham had attacked first and that she'd drawn a weapon on her. Lucky for her, the classroom she was in had a camera, and after the video was watched several times, the woman was carted off to jail. Graham was sent home with an ice pack and a stern warning that things would be reviewed. Whatever the hell that meant.

Teaching wasn't her first choice of jobs to do. Not that she really needed to work—there was plenty of money if she wanted to become a lady of leisure—but she wasn't cut out for that sort of thing. Neither was her dad, and he was a good deal older than her. Going into their home, a modest looking little thing from the outside, she felt much better. Her dad was just pouring them both a cup of tea when she joined him in the kitchen.

"I spoke with young Laci and Max today. My goodness, they have such good heads on their shoulders." Graham said nothing, wondering not for the first time why anyone cared about the Lannings any more as they all knew that Sonya was dead. "Max has been helping her with the magic she got from the safe I left her. I just knew it was going to be a bit much for the young couple."

"Dad, I'm sure that she's going to be just fine." Her magic stirred around her and she looked around for the source of her unease. "Did you change something here?"

"No. I've been out until a little bit ago. I was working in the yard." He sipped his tea and looked at her over the rim. "You have blood on your lip."

Her magic stirred again and she realized what it was as soon as the doorbell rang. Neither of them went to answer it. They didn't know many people that would come to see them, and they didn't like salesmen. This particular salesperson had been to their door before and had been warned. They did not buy steaks from the back of a truck. With a small zap to his ass, the man finally left them. As did her magic warning her.

After telling her dad about her day, she got up to make them some dinner. The house, for all its smallness on the outside, was much larger inside. There were four bedrooms, four and a half baths, as well as an exercise room, living room, and a kitchen large enough to hold both a place for them to create their magic, as well as a nook to fix meals and eat. From the outside the house looked to be a single bedroom home on a single floor plan. She loved it here, and the quietness of the surrounding area.

"That reminds me, the school called here just a moment ago. They would like to speak to you about the young man's grades. I do believe that they're going to ask you to change them to something more suited to a child with some sort of effort involved. In the interest of not having a scandal, is what she said." She just stared at him as he continued. "Also, they wanted you to take a few days off. Just to simmer down. Their words, not mine."

She sat down hard. Not that she didn't expect this to happen, but it still came as a shock to know that her ability as a teacher was so underrated. Not just her, it seemed, but all teachers. And her feelings on having to change Howie's grades didn't change as she sat there and thought about the way his mother had bullied her.

"He doesn't even try to get good grades, Dad. He has it in his head that if they're not right, his mom will come in and save the day. She has in the past, so he knows it will work. And even she knows that if she throws her little tantrum as well as her weight around, she'll get what she wants too. Obviously. Why not keep using what you know works?" Her dad told her he was sorry. "I am as well. I have all these kids that are struggling to keep up, and he just sits in the back of the room and naps. And when he's not doing that, he eats. How are we supposed to help them when they don't even help themselves?"

"I don't know, love. I just don't know." He ate his sandwich and grinned at her. "How about you and me, we try and look at something better. Happier. Would you like to go on a trip with me? You've nothing holding you here now."

"Dad, I'm not going to go and see the Lannings with you. You said yourself that they're doing just fine. I don't want to go and see some overprivileged people that I don't care about or know." He huffed at her. "You know as well as I do that Sonya is no longer a threat to them. So why do you even bother checking up on them?"

"She's no longer a threat, no, but the man that is after them is." She had heard this story so many times she could recite it word for word. "They're not out of danger until they're all mated. They must be mated or things will fall apart again and again until things are set right. The last of them, the second oldest, he needs his mate there with him so that this vicious circle will end."

"And how will you visiting them make that happen?" She shoved her sandwich away, no longer hungry. "Dad, I love you so much and I know that you've been helping them in small ways for a very long time. Also that you feel slightly guilty that you did what you did in the first place by helping Sonya. But I think you've more than made up for it by now with the safe. You set it up so that every time she opens the door, more treasure appears. I think that having it taken from Sonya's estate was a stroke of brilliance too. But they're doing fine. You said so yourself, many times. Just let them go."

"I can't." She wanted to throw up her hands in defeat. Her dad was like a dog with a bone. He would get it down to where he wanted it even if it took several lifetimes to do so. "There are babies born to the women now. Little boys, and some little girls

24

coming along soon too. I want to see them. Know that because of what we've done, they're here despite what that terrible woman had done to them."

"What you've done, not me." The phone ringing had her turning to it. Reaching into it to touch the person on the other end, she knew who it was and what they were going to tell her. "The school. They're telling me that my teaching services are no longer needed. Bastards."

"Good. We will leave here in an hour and have ourselves an adventure." When she growled low, he laughed at her. "You'll love it. And we'll see how all our hard work has paid off. We'll take a few of our old things too, just so that we don't come empty handed. I'm sure that pretty little antique store could use a few things that we no longer have any use for."

As he walked away, still talking, she got up from her chair. She knew that she was going to end up going with him, but that didn't mean that she had to be happy about it. Her dad was her world and she would do anything for him. And he knew it. Answering the phone, Graham let them tell her that she was no longer employed for causing a ruckus. Also that Howie had proof that he had the grades needed to have them changed. She just hung up on the principal.

~~~

Rider felt his cat stretch out on the ground and felt the calmness of him all the way to his bones. This was the way things should be when on a much needed vacation. A working one, but much more fun than he'd anticipated. He looked up when his mom came out of the hotel they were staying in and looked down at him.

"You should be more careful, Rider. What if someone sees you?" He looked over the deck railing where he was and at the expansive waters in front of him. Beyond that were trees as thick as his at home. "I guess you're right. Who would see a thing but the birds?"

She sat down on one of the chairs that were on the deck and sighed heavily. He knew that she was missing home. He was as well, but they were having fun too. Sitting up, he laid his head on her lap and was happy when she rubbed her fingers through his fur.

"They're having a party tonight." He asked her who, barely paying any attention when she curled her fingers around his ear and scratched. "The family. It's for the opening tomorrow. I know that we're going to pop in to be with them on that, but I'd love to go and be there tonight."

So why don't you? He nearly scratched her when she jerked his fur up so she could look at him. *Mom? You're hurting me.*

"I'm going to do it. Just pop right in there, and you're going with me." He'd started to shake his head when she jerked it up and down by his fur. "You're going with me. I don't remember asking you."

But we've got plans for in the.... He could see the heartbreak on her face. Feel it almost. She really wanted him to go with her. *All right, but we're not taking the cargo van. When we pop in, we're going to have to come back here to drive it home again. At least one of us will. Since we've paid for the hotel, no one will care if it's here overnight.*

"Fine. You can come with one of your brothers." She stood up. "Oh Rider, thank you for this. Sina is going to be so excited too. She said she wants to be there for the family. And Laci did say that I could work the floor with her if she needed me. I don't think she has any idea how successful her little shop is going to be. Did you know that they had to hire someone to watch over little Kelly while this is going on? I might have to convince her

26

RIDER

that he needs to be there too. That way I can sneak peeks at him all day long. Oh, thank you so much for suggesting this, Rider. Thank you."

Rider said nothing; he knew when he'd been had.

When he was alone again, he reached out to Misha to let him know what was going on. They'd be home tonight, he told him, and they'd have to bring the van home in a couple of days, if that was all right.

Of course it is. And maybe I'll tag along with you when you do. I'm needing to stretch my own legs for a bit. After going so long without time off, it's hard to get used to not working at all other than the businesses here. Rider told him he was enjoying himself. *I am too, but you can only sit on your ass for so long before the cat in us gets a little restless. I'm not as bored as I had been, not nearly, but I'm thinking that once the shops open up, it's going to mean more down time.*

Rider had no idea why, but like his mom, he thought this was just going to be the beginning. Even if only one of the businesses took off, they'd have to be going for more items to put in the stores. Charlie's business alone was going to create a constant battle to find fresh and new things to put in her baskets. Even as successful as she had been before she'd married his brother, her business had nearly tripled in the last month. Yes, Rider thought, this was only the beginning.

After he made some arrangements to get the van back home, he laid on the balcony for a bit longer. He wasn't ready to go home just yet, he thought. Yes, he missed his family, but he felt like he was the odd man out most of the time now that they'd found their mates. He didn't enjoy the thought that they might be feeling sorry for him.

No one had ever said anything to him about being single. He knew it was all his thoughts and insecurities. He also knew that

27

someday he'd find her. But for now, he thought it safer for her to be away, at least until they found the last man hunting for her. Rider knew that the way that his luck ran, they'd meet with her dying in his arms. Again, with more fear than he should have been feeling, Rider thought he was going to be alone forever.

Rider had money—plenty of it, as a matter of fact—even before he'd been given his part of the vast estate that came to him when Linyah had come into their lives. He'd not been one to spend money on silly things like cars and such. And now that he had more money than ten generations could spend in all their lives, nothing had changed. He was still very tight with every penny he had.

Stretching out and going into the hotel, he saw his mom packing things in her luggage. He supposed there was nothing he could say to her to change her mind, and made his way to his room. Shifting, he dressed himself and pulled out his luggage.

By the time he was at his home, his luggage traveling with him, he was exhausted. He supposed that exhaustion wasn't really what he felt so much as disappointment. He really wished he was good at haggling with the vendors on items. He was pretty sure that he was getting a good deal anyway, but he knew he could have done better. But he'd see his family again and that made it worthwhile. As he loaded up some of the few things he'd been able to stuff in his bags, he was ready to go to Andrew's home.

He noticed the strange car in the drive, an older automobile that looked as pristine as it had been when it rolled off the line, and smiled. If Laci had gotten it for the shop to park out front, it was going to be epic. Rider had a feeling that men from all over would be there just to get a chance to look at it. Going into the house, he was nearly bowled over by Max and his puppy.

"We were just going out. Grandma is here too. She's in the living room with Grandma Sina." Rider asked about the car. "Oh, some old guy with his daughter. You should go and meet them. The girl is pretty."

He made his way to the kitchen, avoiding the living room all together. As soon as he entered, he nearly turned and left when he saw the commotion going on in there. Food, drinks, as well as people, seemed to be in every square inch of the place. Then he saw the older man.

"Hello." Rider nodded, but didn't take the hand that was offered. "Yes, I can understand your hesitation. Nildale was just telling me about how he'd done some harm to the lady of this house. You must be Rider. How wonderful it is to meet you after all this time."

"I am. And you are?" The man told him. "Allister? Why does that name seem so familiar to me?"

The man laughed and said that he was the Allister of the safe. Rider said that it didn't help, and when he snagged a pizza roll from the tray on the butcher block, his favorite snack, it hit him. And when it did, he nearly swallowed the roll whole.

"There, there, now. You're going to be just fine." Allister was pounding him on the back hard enough to break ribs, but the roll finally dislodged enough that he could breathe again. And when he sat down, a glass of water in his hands, he looked up at the man. "I can see from the expression on your face that you know me now."

"The man in the mirror." He nodded. "You helped my sister-in-law, Laci, with her magic. Well, not helped, but you gave her a bit more than she had. And enough funding to do some pretty amazing things. Did she tell you what she did with it? There are a lot of people now that have money in their accounts that might not have but for that. Thank you very much."

"I did. And what she did with the money had nothing to do with me. I'm glad to hear that she used it for good. Laci—all of the Lannings actually, are very wonderful people. I knew that she'd not use it on herself, and it was easy to let her have it. And the magic has helped her out a bit here and there too. The things that she finds, the older pieces, they know to call to her." Allister asked if he'd like to join him on the deck. With a short nod, Rider not only found himself there with the man, but a plate of food and drinks in front of them both. "You're the last of them, the last Lanning to find your mate, aren't you?"

"Yes, and I will find her. I've not found her yet, but I do know that she's out there. I was sort of hoping that she'd stay away, at least for a little while. If you know about her and me then you know that there is someone still planning to kill her. And us. We still have no new leads on the man that is after her, or what he might do to her when he finds her. I'm pretty sure that he's watching her so that he can intercept her when she gets here." Allister nodded. "Even though I have no idea who or where she is, I still want her safe."

"Commendable, very much so, but I can tell you that he didn't see her." Rider nodded, then looked at the man when he realized what he'd said. "Yes, she's here. In the flesh, so to speak. Not that either one of you are going to be happy about the turn of events, but I kept her safe for you both."

"You know her?" Allister nodded and smiled. Rider wasn't sure why, but he didn't care for that look. "Are you sure she's safe? I mean, you said that this guy, whoever he is, didn't see her, but is she safe from him?"

"Oh yes. My goodness, yes. But right now, so you know, he's sort of out of touch with things going on here. You could say that because of magic, he's not sure what is up." Rider asked him what he meant. "I'm not at my home so he's trying to figure out where I've gotten to. It's a game we play, or I play with him. I disappear for a few days and he gets all wonky. He's not very smart, I don't think. I know that some of the monsters out there, the ones that come for people like me, they can feel me when I'm in the public eye. Today, we took a chance to come here, but it's time. I'm sorry for it."

"Time?" Allister nodded and laughed. "I'm afraid that I don't understand. Time for what? Are you saying that the man will come here soon? Today?"

"Not today, no. But soon after. You're about as prepared as you can be, I suppose, but he'll still get around you if you let him." Rider wasn't sure what the man was talking about and told him that. "Of course you don't. And for that I'm profoundly sorry. But the man, his name eludes me at the moment, he's coming, and very soon. And when he gets here, even with the army that you have at your beck and call, he will still breach your home and get to your mate. Again, if you allow him."

"No. I won't allow that." Allister said it wasn't going to be his fault if it did happen. But his mate was very stubborn. "It will be my fault if he gets to my mate. She's going to be my world, and if she hurts, I will kill him."

"I'm very glad to hear you thinking like that. It makes me feel like this was all worthwhile. I've given up a great deal to come here, to this time." Rider told him he was sorry that he wasn't enjoying himself. "Oh. But I am. I meant coming to this time frame. Do you have any idea how hard it's been to acclimate myself to your strange ways? Not to mention all the changes that I've missed. No gradual buildup of things like technology or diseases and such. Just a slap in the face change. Yes, it was hard.

31

The thing I missed.... Well, there are cars and televisions, which I will admit I never cared for. Also music. You cannot fathom the changes in that. Then there is—"

"I'm sorry, but I have no idea what you're talking about." Allister nodded and then looked at him with a sad smile. "Would you like for me to call someone? Max said that you have a daughter. Would you like for me to call her for you?"

"Nay, she comes now." Rider nodded but kept an eye on the elderly man. He had thought when he'd first seen him that he was in his late sixties. But now, on closer inspection, he could see that he was much older. Like pushing eighty or older. "There she is now."

The sliding door behind him opened and Rider stood up. He wasn't prepared, his mind told him, not for her. Not for the beauty that came out into the sunlight. Then she smiled at the elderly man and Rider had to grab the back of the chair or simply fall over. Christ, she was a vision.

"Dad, you wanted me?" So did Rider, but he didn't say anything. He knew that their need for the woman was nothing alike. "I thought you were going to get the things out of the car and we'd be on our way."

"No." Rider felt his face heat up when they both looked at him. "What I meant was, you can't leave just yet. My mom would love to meet you both."

Rider had a feeling that he'd been set up. Not by his mom, but by the man with him. When Allister laughed and said that he'd love to meet her as well, Rider nodded, feeling well out of his normal self. His cat started to give him a hard time as well when Allister reached over and hugged the woman.

"Graham, this is Rider Lanning. The last of the Lanning men to find his mate." She didn't put out her hand but Rider wanted it, to touch some part of her now. "Rider, this is my daughter, Graham. We adopted the last name of Taylor when we first came here, but we don't really have one."

"Where did you come from?" When Allister didn't answer him, Rider had to work hard to pull his eyes away from Graham when he laughed. "I don't know what's going on here."

"Of course you do. You've met my daughter, and you know as well as I do that she's your other half."

Rider felt himself get dizzy, his legs weaken. When he was seated, his head between his knees, he could hear them arguing. Christ, all he could think of was his brothers telling him that his mate was going to give him a very hard time. It seemed that they were going to be correct and he was never going to live this down.

CHAPTER 3

Allister waited until the man seemed to be stronger before he sat down with him. Things were out of his hands now; his daughter was with Rider. She was safe, his mind kept telling him, but his heart was breaking. His daughter had her mate and she no longer needed him.

"Dad, what the hell have you done?" He looked at her when she spoke to him. So lovely, even when she was upset like this. "Did you do this? Arrange for me to be his mate?"

"Don't be daft, girl. I could no more do that than I could change your mind about bringing me here. He's your mate, has been since the beginning of time." He looked over at Rider and wondered if the man was going to be good for his little girl. He certainly looked to be well out of his element at the moment. Then he remembered what he'd seen of this man, and realized she'd be better with Rider than she'd ever been with him.

"You need to explain to me what you've done." Allister nodded at the younger man. Knowing that this was going to be hard on them all, Rider asked Graham to let Allister finish his

35

story before judging him. Allister laughed when she sat on the deck floor rather than take the chair next to Rider. "I'm not going to hurt you, Graham, you know that. If we're mates, and I have no reason to not believe him, then you know that I could no more harm you than I could my own mom."

"No, you're not going to hurt me. You're not going to do a lot of things that might be going on in that male chauvinistic head of yours. I'm not going to be your mate." Allister had been looking at Rider and saw the pain there, the hurt, and felt sorry for the man. His daughter was strong, stubborn, and smart. But he knew Rider was all that and more. "Explain, Dad. Why did you send me here?"

"Sonya knew who you were. Not just that you were stronger than her; any fool could see that she wasn't anything at all when it came to magic. But that you were a key to her taking down the Lannings." Rider asked how that was to work. "You mean because she was born in a different century? We're the same as you. Immortal. But unlike you, we can be killed easily. Well, not easily, but there aren't as many rules to be followed just to remove my head. Just a blade to my throat and that's all it would take. But Sonya had made several plans in regards to taking down your family. And Graham was going to be the magical push she needed to end you all."

"Sonya was going to kill you after you did what she wanted with the safe, right? I'm assuming that she would have killed Graham too, had you not sent her here. It's a brilliant plan, but as you know, it did little to stop her madness. Unless you know more than we do on this." Allister nodded at Rider. "Christ, even dead this woman is more trouble than she was worth. And the safe? The money? Your doing as well, I'm assuming? For your daughter or the fool?"

"Neither, as a matter of fact. They were going to Laci. I knew in my heart after meeting her that she'd do a lot of good with the things in the safe. I also knew that I'd need the connection to her, just to keep tabs on the family, and she worked out better than I had planned. Sonya had set up the safe, of course, but she never knew the power I had to go to and fro in between the times, and I saw things that.... Well, after seeing things work, how things were going, I came back and forth through different times to set things up for my daughter. Made investments and plans for her. I hadn't planned to come along with her. But I did end up here as well." Rider looked at Graham and seemed to know it was her doing. "She didn't know why I sent her here. I did that on my own. I needed her to be safe, from Sonya and that man that seeks to end her life."

"Of course you did. I would have done the same had it been my child." Rider looked back at him as he continued. "Sonya had you put the money, jewels, and magic together so that whoever killed us off, they'd get it. Is that correct?"

"Oh no, that's.... Well, the money and jewels, yes. Those were her idea. And there was to be a particular kind of magic. It was only enough for him to know to go to her when he had accomplished the task she set before him. The person who got the safe open was to become her mate, you see. A man that would stand beside her through time. He was to become beautiful with the magic there, well-endowed, as well as strong enough to.... She had tastes, you see. Tastes that would kill a lesser man. I have no idea why she thought that might work, but if you ever met her, you'd know she wasn't all that smart. But that wasn't what I put there."

"I see." When Rider glanced at Graham again, Allister thought of the two of them together. His daughter and this man would make wonderful children. Strong too. "But you knew that Laci would get it. So you adjusted things so that she'd be able to use the magic there as well as the funds."

"Yes. I saw all of you. I wanted to see first of all why Sonya wanted you dead and what sort of people you were. I came back several times over the years to watch your family. Hannah and her babe being born. Your relationship with the king and queen. I even saw you. But there was something keeping me from seeing into your mind. I couldn't see your future, find out what your worth was, but could only observe you. I wished to leave the safe to you and all the magic within, but I could not." Rider said nothing, but Allister had a feeling that he knew the reason. It was because of the hold on his mind. From a far stronger person than he'd ever be. "So when I saw that Laci was going to be in my home, far in the future of course, I decided that I'd give her the magic. Especially after I saw that she had the gift of touch."

"You mean where she can see the people that owned or used any object she touched?" Allister nodded and smiled. "I don't think she appreciated all that you gave her as much as you might think. And I'm sure that her mate wouldn't be happy with you either if it hadn't done so much good for so many people."

"No. It was a great deal. And had it been you, as I wanted, then it wouldn't have harmed you nearly as much. But as I have said, I wasn't able to hand it off to you." Allister looked at his daughter when she stood up. As she paced, thinking hard, he knew, he continued with his tale. "Sonya was going to behead my daughter after she'd finished with her. Simply because she was your mate. So like a good father, I lied to her. I told her that she'd been burned at the stake, dead to me. It was one of the hardest things I've ever done, to lie to the woman. While her magic was weak, there was still pain from going against her."

"You should have told me." Allister said he knew that now but had been afraid. "Of her or me? Because I could have helped you with her."

"Yes, but at what cost?" Graham looked at him and he could see she was understanding, even just a little of what he'd done. "Had I not sent you here, you would have been killed. I knew what her plans for me were, and they were no less horrid. But it was something I was willing to do, just to save you. I could see it in her mind. While she wasn't very smart, she had no problems killing those that had served her purpose. I could not die without doing something, anything, that I could to save you."

~~~

Getting up, his head still swimming, Rider held tightly onto the table. He wasn't sure if it was to keep himself from running or because he was dizzy. Graham continued to pace but she was quiet now, understanding, he'd bet, what had led her father to do what he'd done. Love was a very powerful motivator. Rider still wasn't sure how this had worked, Graham being here and his mate, but he knew as surely as he was standing there that she was.

"This person, this monster, you call him...do you know who he is?" They both turned to him and he sat down again. "Please. Let's just be calm and collected and try to figure out what has happened here. And how we can be safe."

Allister frowned at him then looked at Graham. "I don't know the man that comes for her. I know that he is here, in this time, but what he has magically is beyond my knowledge." He looked at Rider then. "She will be safe here. And once you have come together, his job will be over. There will be nothing for him to do when you become mates."

"I am not his mate and I would appreciate it if you'd stop

saying that." Rider watched her pace, not like she was thinking, but more that it was her job and she was going to be the best at it. "I was just fine where I was, in a time that I completely understood. Then one day you put me thousands of years ahead of my time, and now you tell me it was a trick."

"He didn't tell you it was a trick. He simply said—" When she looked at him, daggers seemingly shooting from her eyes, he smiled at her. "You're the most beautiful creature I've ever seen. And your eyes? They're gorgeous."

"Don't. I don't want you being nice to me or complimenting me or anything else to me." His mind took a hard twist, thinking of all the other things he'd like to be doing to her. "Stop that. Damn it, this isn't going to happen. I am not your mate. I don't even like you."

"That's not terribly fair, is it? You don't even know me." She sat down finally and Rider sat on his hands rather than reach for hers. He had an overwhelming need to touch her, but thought she'd hurt him if he did. "You said that a monster is looking for her and that he knows that you're not at home. I'm assuming this person knows you, but not her."

"Yes. He finds me out and about, not often but he does. He cannot harm me; I've no idea why, not as yet, but I think we'll find out now." Rider glanced at Graham while Allister explained. "Sonya came to me. Told me all the names of those who were to die by her hand and her reasons behind it. She wanted to be queen and thought.... Well, I'm not sure what her thinking was, but she felt that if Kendra's sister was dead that Kendra would step down and Sonya would be crowned the queen. I never saw a woman so set on something that was so far out of her reach than it was for her. I wrote them all down, searched for them through the ages, and made sure, with just a little help from another being, that they stayed alive to be friends with you. I watched over my daughter myself."

"But Sonya is dead." Rider told Graham that she was. "So I don't understand. The money and magic has been given away. The leader is dead. Why would this person continue to try and finish up her plans when there is neither a reward nor anyone around that would care? And this does not mean I'm all for this mating business. I want answers, not a mate."

"I don't believe that whoever this person is has any idea that the magic or reward, whatever he was promised, is gone. He more than likely knows that Sonya is dead. I think, with some of the information we've been able to find, that she supplied these men, others that have long since been killed, with not just money to get them to this point, but magic as well. I don't know as yet if their magic disappeared when she was killed, but I'm thinking not." Rider looked at Graham. "Your father sent you to this time frame to save you. As for being my mate? I don't know how that works. But you are. And I'm pretty sure you know it."

"What I know is that you're not going to claim me simply because someone says so." Linyah came out onto the deck then and leaned against the railing, not saying a word. Rider wasn't surprised by her quiet demeanor, but apparently it bothered Graham. She stood up and faced the genjar like she was going to harm her. "You think you're going to make me be his mate? I have news for you, you just don't want to fuck with me."

"I have no desire to fuck with you in any shape or form." He nearly laughed when Graham's face turned a brilliant shade of red. "I'm here simply because Rider belongs to me."

"Then you can have him." When Graham started to pace again, she stilled and Rider could see that Linyah had tensed up as well. "Someone is out there."

41

Her voice was low, not soft, but hard. When Linyah told Rider to sit down, he did so without hesitation. Allister didn't move either, but closed his eyes and took Graham's hand into his.

"There is a being out there. I cannot tell what he is." Linyah answered Allister's question quietly. "Yes, I see that now. He is all. There are creatures with him, two that are beside him, three more that are surrounding the area."

"All?" Graham answered Rider's question. "You mean that he's every paranormal. Then shifter, right?"

"Nay, he is all, yet not one. A shifter would have to change into another being. He could take on the appearances of a vampire, but he would not be one. He could be a leopard, but he would only look like you. He is all and more." Rider nodded, but his mind wasn't accepting what Linyah was telling him. "Magical too. I can almost taste his strength."

"He is moving away. I think he is aware that we can see him." Rider didn't know if that was a good thing or not and asked Graham. "It's hard to say. I know that he's frustrated because he cannot breach this area. His men—one has been killed. The pack that roams here, they've found him and killed him."

"James Luna, pack master." Graham nodded and took his hand. "Christ."

It was like being touched with a live wire that tuned him into everything. It took him several seconds to calm his heart, then to make his eyes adjust to what he was seeing. His ability to see far off was there as a leopard, but now he could see bugs on plants, see the flutter of the trees miles away that were hidden deep in the forest.

Concentrate on the ground. You'll see it then. He looked downward, his stomach not liking the way things moved in and out. *Don't jerk around. Just look like you would if you were standing right on top of it.*

The ground was darker in spots. He realized that he was looking at footprints. Following them, he saw the men and moved closer, keeping his eye on the things around him too. Graham told him that he wasn't there, he didn't need to move like he was. Understanding dawning, he moved ahead of the man and turned to see his face.

I know him. Graham asked him from where. *I'm not sure just yet. There is too much going on for me to think. But I do. The men with him, I don't know them, but I would be able to recognize them should I see them again.*

Describe him for me. Rider made his body, or however he was seeing the man, move backward as the man continued on his way. *Don't let him touch you, Rider. I don't know what will happen if you do.*

He has a scar on his face. From his left eye...no, it's his right eye to his cheek. His lips are puckered as well. Like he'd been stitched back together hastily, and not well. Graham told him to continue. *Dark hair. He doesn't appear to be tall, less than six foot. Stocky build, but not muscled. Like maybe at one time he'd been stronger but he's let himself go. He has a mark on his hand. Let me look.*

Before he could get too close to him, the man stopped. And when he did, Rider did as well. As the man looked around, so did he. Rider realized almost too late that he didn't have to worry about whatever had startled the man, and looked at his hand. Then the man was gone.

Opening his eyes, Rider looked at Graham. She still held his hand so he curled his fingers into hers and held her. He was overwhelmed, his mind still swirling around what he'd done. And when she sat down hard, he realized that whatever they'd shared had taken a great deal out of her. He watched her while he told them what he'd seen.

"The mark is of a circle with a large dragon in the center. The wings are curled around the body, but his tail is touching the circle it's within. It moved…the dragon moved, opening its eyes, and looked at me before he spread his wings and nodded his head." Linyah asked him the color. "Purple. As brilliantly purple as Graham's eyes are."

When no one spoke, he looked at Linyah. Her father had joined her at some point, as had her mom. They were staring at him as if he'd done something horribly wrong and he stood up. Rider pulled Graham to him and held her, thankful that she didn't try to get away from him. He asked what was going on.

"The keeper of the dragon." Sina sat down then stood up. When she seemed to collapse in the chair again, Nildale held her hand while she continued. "Many centuries ago, more than I can even remember, there were dragons aplenty. We have them now, a few for show, but there were so many that they would darken the sky when they took to flight."

"This man, he had to do with why there are so few now?" Sina shook her head and Rider watched as tears rolled down her cheeks. "You know who this is though, don't you?"

"Yes. His name is Shadow, or so it was then. He is…was the man who trained the dragons to let riders sit upon their backs, know when to fire upon a village or whatever we needed, and to work with us in other ways as well. Shadow and his men saved us a great many times when we were just starting out." Nildale sat down with his wife but continued to hold her as Sina spoke. "When we were at peace, our lands and people so few that we were no longer considered a threat, Shadow put his dragons to sleep, sharing the magic that he used to do so. But the grand

44

dragon, the one that sired them all, had been killed. Or so he told us."

"Wait. You're saying that this mark has something to do with this grand dragon? That the mark is telling us that he's alive out there somewhere? And that he can use him against the Lannings?" Sina shook her head at Graham. "But it is something, right?"

"The dragon is there, on his skin." Rider asked her what she meant. "He has somehow pulled the dragon to his body. It's what he is, it's how he is all, as Allister said. The dragon is powerful and has his own magic, so since he is within the body of the man, he would take on most if not all of his magic too. He would be all of it. Shadow has somehow captured him, wears him on his skin so that he can use him against us all. And he will unless the dragon's owner releases him from the circle."

Everyone turned to Graham. Her eyes were darkened now, the purple of them nearly black. Rider had a thought, one that scared him more than he could say, but when Graham looked at him he could see that she was thinking the same thing.

"The dragon is somehow connected to me. And more than likely Rider too. That's why we're called together as mates." Sina told her that's what she had surmised as well. "And this man, you think he knows that? That Rider and I are supposed to be mates and that he has the dragon's magic to kill us with it?"

"I believe so, yes. It might explain why he's waited so long to come for you. He needed you to be with the Lannings when the time came to kill them all. Having a dragon loose in this world for any amount of time would be risky. He'd have to have him released and then kill him almost immediately after everyone was taken care of so as no one would know what happened." Graham asked Nildale how hard it would be to kill the dragon.

"For him? Not so hard. Remember, he is a part of the dragon and he'd only have to order it to death. But he needs you here as well. Without you, he cannot release the dragon. It's your magic and that of Rider that will have to do the deed. And once released, he would control him. As his trainer, he knows that the dragon would have no choice but to obey him."

Rider didn't know what to think. A dragon was here? To destroy them all? He tried to think how that would work, how a dragon could kill them all and be so small. And he was small. No bigger than a dime, he thought. When he had his thoughts in order to ask, he looked around and saw that it was just he and Linyah on the deck; the others had left.

"She's your mate, you are aware of this?" He nodded at her. "I hold you, Rider. And I can only give you to her when she accepts you. You belong to me. As for the rest, Allister not being able to get into your head, that is my doing as well."

"You told me that before. I still am no closer to figuring out what that meant than I was back then." She leaned back in her seat and put out her hand. Before he could take it, thinking that was her intent, an image appeared in her hand. "That's me."

"It is, yes. And if you will be kind enough to watch, I can show you why it was important for me to hold you." While he watched the image, he saw himself on a job. The one that they'd gone to months before they'd closed down. "The man that you were talking to, do you see him there? Had you not been mine, this is what might have happened to you."

As he watched, the man pulled a gun and shot Rider in the chest four times. Then in the head. When he fell backwards, his body riddled with holes, Linyah was there. Then he was standing again, talking to the man and nothing happened. The next image was of him in a large body of water. He was dressed in a wet suit helping out by searching for bodies. Before he could remember that event and put a name to it, a large log popped up from the depths and hit him in the head, removing it from his shoulders. But again, Linyah was there, and the scene changed to one where he wasn't touched by the log, and he continued with what he'd been doing.

"I thought we were unable to be killed unless there were all these rules in place." She stared at him. "Linyah, why is this showing me dying when I was told we couldn't be killed?"

"You belong to me." He nodded. "You will never die. No one will ever be able to remove your head, with or without the rules. If a person were to cut you now you'd live. If someone were to put you to a guillotine, you'd live. No one will be able to ever end your life but me."

"I don't understand. Why would you do that?" Instead of answering him, she picked up his hand and flipped it over. There on the back of his hand was the dragon. As he watched it, the wings spread out and he seemed to be bowing to him once again. He was almost afraid to ask, but he really needed to know. "Does Graham have one as well?"

"Yes. As of the moment you touched her, you both had the magic given to you."

Rider watched the dragon as it moved over his skin, up his arm to his wrist. "You knew this was going to happen when you touched me that day."

"No. I knew that I had to protect you above all others. Why, I had no idea, but that's what I knew." He asked her who had told her. "I'm sure you know as well as I do who that might have been. Nic seems to have an inside to a great many things. By the way, he's the other being that has helped your family along to get to this point. And since he asked me to do this, I did. I just didn't know why."

"So just as I was being killed by the log and the man, you came back, erased that time, and fixed it." When she didn't answer, he looked up at her. "Tell me, Linyah. How many times have you come to save my life?"

"Thousands."

CHAPTER 4

Graham wasn't sure what she should do. Staying away from the man that would claim her was a priority, of course, but other than that she had no set plans. There wasn't any way for her to go home now, she knew that as well. The man would rain a hell onto these people that would be her fault. She needed to be there to protect them. And her dad.

"Hello." Graham looked at the young boy that sat down with her. He was handsome, and she knew right away what he was. "Yes. And you know what I can do as well. And since I have a lot of studying to do for my final tests, I think we can dispense with the niceties and get on with it. I've come to answer your questions." He grinned, such a boyish thing to do, and she was disarmed by it. And charmed.

"There are just too many for me to sort out right now to even form any questions." He nodded and handed her a plate of cookies. They were macaroons, her favorite. Taking two, she picked up the glass of tea that had appeared when the cookies did. "You?"

"Yes. You're stressed. And while cookies don't solve everything, they can make a person feel better. I think it's the art of chewing, or concentrating on it. Something like that." She nodded and ate two more before he spoke again. "My name is Max Lanning. My mom is Murph. You've met her and my grandmother, so you know just what we are."

"Doran." He grinned and nodded at her. "You're also the owner of the pup that is now in the yard and not the house because he peed on the carpet. He smells of you."

"He knows better, but he was nervous. You made him nervous. I don't think you will now, not now that you've been marked, but still, the damage was done." She pulled her sleeve over the mark that she'd noticed an hour ago. "Do you know what that means? We can start there if you wish."

"No, I don't know what it means. Not all of it. I know that somehow I have this connection to the dragon that I share with Rider. What kind of connection to the dragon, I have no idea. But I have a feeling that you do." He nodded. "Also, that somehow the only way I can complete this connection to this creature is to take Rider as my mate."

"No. You have the connection already. It's not complete, as you said, but you have it. Rider will make it stronger for you. You both play a part in his life, and together you can help him." She had figured that out as well. "He's trapped there, against his will."

"I would think that anyone being trapped, it would be against their will." He grinned again. "This man, he knew I'd come here. That I'd be with the Lannings too, didn't he?"

"Yes. He has been watching. I'm not sure if he knows who you are—there are several women on this estate—but he knows that one of them is who he must have to release the dragon." She asked him if there was any way to change his mind. "I don't think so. And even if you could, there is more than just this man and the dragon involved. Much more. It's a paradox. He must have you to release the dragon to kill the family. But if he kills you, he cannot complete the task that was set before him, which is, again, to kill the dragon. This thing, his job, was created so long ago that no one might remember the reason why. So his timing must be perfect. I'm not sure how his timeline works, but I do know that things must be done correctly. So if the dragon is not released, the timeline fulfilled, then the circle of the Lannings' lives, and yours, will have to be restarted. At some other time frame in life, and with others playing the parts. Understand?"

"We've done this before, haven't we? All of us; myself, the other women, the Lannings. Some of us have found our mates, while others, the brothers or the women they were to love, were killed or died. And each time the circle isn't completed, we have to do it again and again. Don't you think that's a little sick? To kill off some people to have a dragon released?" He told her that it wasn't just the dragon, but happiness for them all. "I see. So, without this, all of this, the world comes to an end?"

"Not an end, no, but you know as well as I that there are many people that can be affected by the death of a single person. If say, my mom would have died that day, or Laci hadn't come to the family, there wouldn't be justice for a great many people in need." She frowned at him, not getting it. "Laci found the money, as you know. And the magic. Her helping others, a great many of them, has enriched the lives of children, adults, and the land. Simply because she gave them a helping hand. My mom is there to save the innocent. Some of them aren't so innocent, as you know, but they play a part — all of us do to the end — of something huge. Every day, we touch the lives of people and make a difference.

Not always a good one, but a difference all the same."

"Did my father know this?" Max told her no, he was only saving his child. "And had I stayed where I'd been born, what would have happened to me?"

"You'd be dead. Sonya would have taken you to her home. She would have murdered you, not gently, but you'd be just as dead. Then your father. He would have suffered greatly for his part in her plan, simply because she murdered you in his presence." Graham nodded. "Rider will never harm you. You know that."

"Yes. I mean, I know how having a mate works. Someone... whoever has decided that we're to be together, but just in case it doesn't really work out, they made it so that we can't harm each other. Kinda fucked up if you ask me. It's sort of like taking out a pre-nup because you figure there isn't any way that the two of you will ever work things out."

"Andy Lanning was Rider's father. You will not have known him, nor he you, but he was a part of their lives until recently. Maribel, my grandmother, was his mate. He abused her, both verbally and physically. The boys too when they were younger. Then one day he told them that he'd had enough. That he no longer wanted them in his life. But it didn't stop him from hurting her every chance he got, as well as taking the very food from his sons' mouths when he thought he deserved it more." She asked him why he'd tell her that. "He harmed his mate, nearly killed her on several occasions. Just because it is written that you can't harm your mate, does not mean that it doesn't happen."

"You think he'll hurt me? Rider, I mean?" Max asked her what she thought. "No. I think he'd die for me, and willingly. I only just met him, but I can feel him. Like he's already a part of me. I know that should it come to it, Rider would die for any of his family and not hesitate a bit."

"The dragon knows this as well." She felt him stir on her then; the dragon moved over her arm. She wondered aloud if the man could feel him as well. "I don't know. The man is not anyone that I've touched, I've had no contact with him, so I can't know his mind. Nor that of the dragon. Only you and Rider can tell that."

"If I stay here, become his mate, what do you think we'll be able to do?" The door opened and she looked up at Rider. He looked as overwhelmed as she felt. "We were just discussing the dragon."

"I've been talking to Linyah about him as well." As he moved onto the deck where they were, Max stood up. "You don't have to leave. I just need to be near her."

"I've told her all I know." Which wasn't true, he'd not really told her anything, Graham thought, but had created more questions. "I have some studying to do as well. I'll be around if you need me."

After Max left them, Rider sat down. Not close enough for her to touch, but she could smell him. She looked around the yard, wondering whose house she was at and why they were all gathered here. She knew it was one of the brothers, but his name wasn't something she remembered right now.

"This is Andrew's home. This is a pre-celebration for the grand opening of our businesses tomorrow. We have three new shops opening in town that we all have a stake in. I was antique hunting with my mom and Sina when we decided to come home for the party." Graham asked him if he wanted her to come back later. "No. Why would I want that?"

"I don't know. My dad and I sort of just showed up here uninvited. And you obviously had plans." He did reach for her hand then, and for some reason that she didn't want to think about, Graham didn't pull away. "I don't know what is going on. There is just too much for me to handle right now. Dragons and magic, mates and men trying to kill me off. It's a lot to think on, don't you think?"

"Yes. I've been trying to sort things out myself. I'm a very detail-oriented person, and this is just too much for me to even know how to write down to sort out. I'm sure we'll get answers, but right now I just want to touch you. And feed you dinner too." Graham asked him what they were having. "My mom is big on trying new things. And even though she wasn't here, I'm sure that some of the things that will be on the table tonight will be of her doing. Last time we had a gathering, we had this God-awful salad dressing that made Andrew sick and Hannah break out in a rash. She's more careful now."

She could smell food now. Steak if she wasn't missing her bet. Pie crust too. And a little bit of cherries in something. Lifting her nose to the air, she thought that she could smell bacon and potatoes, as well as salad dressing. Her belly rumbled in protest of having those scents and nothing filling it.

"May I kiss you?" Graham looked at Rider and thought of how handsome he was. How utterly kind he looked. "Please?"

"It's going to happen, isn't it? That you and I come together and become a couple." He didn't say anything, nor did he nod out his agreement to her. "I don't want this. I don't need or want you in my life. While it's not perfect, it is mine. And my choices to make. I feel run over by decisions that I have no say in. It's like we've been thrown together for no other reason than we serve a purpose. I want love and romance, don't you?"

When Rider let go of her hand and stood up, she felt bereft, cold and lonely. Shaking off the feelings as best she could, she watched him walk to the door and open it. Before she could ask him where he was going, he turned back to her.

"Yes, I want romance and love as well. But I'm sorry you feel that just because we're serving a purpose, that we can't still have those things. While I can understand it, I don't have to like it." He looked into the house before turning back to her. "You have low expectations about this, and to a point I can understand that as well. But unlike you, I'm willing to give it what I can for any time we might have left."

"You're leaving?" He nodded and told her he thought it for the best. "You're just going to run away, leave me here by myself because I'm being honest with you? How mature is that?"

"I would think it's very mature. And I'll be honest with you as well. I don't want you in my life either, not if you don't want to be there. So, if it's all the same to you, I'd very much like it if you'd just leave me to my peace." He moved into the house but looked at her again before leaving. "I'm sorry, Graham, I truly am."

Then he was gone. The door closed so softly behind him that she didn't even hear the latch in the frame connect. He just left her. Even after being told that his family would die, that the dragon would come for them if they didn't come together, he left her there. Standing up, she nearly screamed when a man appeared in front of her.

~~~

The van was just where he'd left it. Digging out the keys, he put them in the lock and opened the door. Rider was going to finish this trip, get some things for the shop, then take a long vacation.

As soon as he started the engine he knew that he wasn't going to take a trip anywhere. Sitting there with his head on the steering wheel, he thought about Graham and what she'd said to him. The sound of the passenger door opening had him looking. To say he was surprised to see Graham there would have been grossly understated.

"We need to talk." He nodded, but didn't say anything. "You can't just say things like that and leave. I deserve the right to have my say as well."

"I was pretty sure that you'd made your opinion on all of this very clear." She said nothing. "Who the hell do I have to kill for bringing you here?"

"I can do a lot of shit too, you know. You're not the only one with the ability to go where you want when you want." He said nothing as she got in the van with him and buckled up. "Where are we headed?"

"I'm not sure this is a good idea. Maybe you should head back to my brother's house and we'll talk when I get back." She was shaking her head. "I don't want you here. I can't have you so near, smelling you and knowing that I can't touch you. Go away."

"I can smell you too." Rider looked out the front window, his anger at this making his cat pissy as well. "Where are we going?"

Putting the van in reverse, he took them out to the road. He was going to do this by not talking to her. He wasn't sure how mature he was being now, but he wasn't going to get close to her, nor was he going to be nice. When she laughed, he looked her way and decided that he didn't like her overly much and said just that to her.

"I don't like you either. You're bossy and a pain in the ass, but I'm having fun and I'm not going to let you rain on my day." He told her what Linyah had told him, not all but most of it. "She owns you? I guess that explains a great deal. However, I'm unsure as to why she'd think I'd care."

"You don't want a thing to do with me, I would imagine." He heard her say something, but not what it might have been. "I'm trying to clear my head, not have some gabby passenger drive me insane all the time. So either sit there and shut up or go back home. I don't care which."

The silence didn't bother him. Rider liked his quiet. He also enjoyed his own company. The radio was off, which was the way he liked it, and he had rolled down the window in deference to the air conditioning. When he was in line again for the roadside flea market, he watched the stalls for items that he wanted.

It was freeing, being here, knowing that he was going to have fun. And even with her there, which he was going to do his level best to ignore, he was going to get some deals and have fun. Alone if need be. When he came upon a group of vendors, he decided that she could come or not, he didn't care.

Pulling over so that he could get out, he didn't bother asking her if she wanted to join him. Seeing three stalls, really just people selling from a wagon and the back of their van, he made his way to them. His list said jars, and he had seen some here.

"How much for the bowl?"

Rider wanted to tell her that it wasn't on his list but wasn't going to engage with Graham. He kept telling himself that she wasn't there, that he didn't have to talk to her. It didn't work, of course, but he told himself that.

When the man told her a price for the bowl, he watched her as she haggled with the man. Rider had tried that a few times, to get the vendor to a lower price, but he'd been so terrible that he just paid the price they said. But he was amazed at the ease with which Graham did it, taking an eight-dollar bowl down to two bucks. He handed her the three blue jars that he wanted.

As they went from vendor to vendor, he wished he'd brought

the wagon that had been in the van. When it was obvious that they needed to dump their things off, he watched Graham purchase an old blanket that he'd not seen, as well as a scale that was too heavy for her to carry. When she picked it up, laughing with the man she'd bought it from, the guy took it from her and carried it to the van for them. After helping her store it in the back, he waved them off when Rider offered him money for the help. When they were alone, he just looked at her.

"You're beautiful. More so when you smile." He nearly fell to his knees when she smiled wider, her face alight with it. Before he could think it wasn't what she wanted, Rider pulled her to him by cupping the back of her head and kissed her.

Honey. Mine. Spice. And Sex. All those and more entered in his mind as he held her body to his. His tongue tasting what she had to offer. And the feeling of her flesh, strong and muscled, as it filled his hand.

When he lifted his head from hers, he saw need there. He had some too, but it was a gentle need, like he could hold her and be content. When she turned from him, reaching for the wagon, Rider wasn't upset, didn't feel like she'd shunned him, but was happy that she was sharing this with him. As they made their way back to the vendors, he took her hand in his as they walked.

"I can't do what you do to get the prices lower. I've been paying full price for things all along." She asked him why not. "I have no idea. I guess I figure that they put that price on things because they think that's what it's worth. The couple of times I tried, I felt like a fool. And didn't get a deal at all."

"I'm glad to know that you don't use your power to read their minds to get what they want out of each piece. Not only would that be wrong, but not nearly as much fun. You do think this is fun, right?" He nodded and told her he loved this. "Me too. I used to do this a long time ago. Not the buyer part, but the vendor. It was more prevalent than it is now. There were food vendors everywhere instead of stores. Dad and I would grow vegetables then sell what we couldn't use. It was stressful for a lot of people, making enough to get by. But Dad and I, we did it to get out of the house."

"I didn't think I'd enjoy shopping for antiques and other items that are about as useful as those jars you picked up. But it's fun, getting a deal for something, the thrill of knowing that you got something that someone else has used, touched, or even tossed out." She told him she loved auctions as well. "That's not my department. Laci can do it and so can Andrew, but I get nervous and overbid."

"You just have to have a set price that you're willing to pay and stick to it." He nodded and picked up some old tools that were on display. "Those are nice. Do you by chance have a list of items we're looking for?"

Handing her the list, he picked up the long blade that was there. He had no idea why but it seemed to call to him. After putting his hand around the handle of it, he felt the strength of it, the magic that surrounded it. And he could see…well, everything. Looking at Graham, he could tell she felt it as well.

"That's only four dollars. To be honest with you, we didn't even know we had it until we were unpacking today." Rider tore his eyes from Graham's and looked at the man speaking. "You want it? How about two dollars? I'll even wrap it up in the burlap it was in."

"Yes, we'll take it. And these." Graham took the blade from him and handed it, along with a few other things, to the man who was behind his makeshift table. "Also, those green and blue jars."

They were standing in front of the van again before he knew

it. When she shoved him in the passenger side, he had to be buckled in as well as his seat put back. They were moving down the road when what had happened hit him.

"We used that. Against the man. Or we did at some point. Did you see that?" She nodded and told him to shut up a minute. "No. I can't. The two of us, we take that knife and we cut that man's head off. Then we take it and—"

The van came to a sudden and violent stop. Graham got out of the seat and was halfway across the dense forest behind the parking lot of a gas station before he caught up to her. As soon as he touched her arm, she came around swinging and caught him in the face with her fist.

He let it take him to the ground, pulling her along with him. As she struggled against his hold, Rider did everything he could to keep her from unmanning him and hitting him again. When she finally tired or just quit, he held her to him.

"I've never killed anyone before." He just held her while she spoke. "I saw us, the two of us, use that knife against the man, and we were both killed because of the dragon getting to us. Just like it was nothing."

"No, it was something." She turned in his arms and looked down at him. "He was trying to kill our family. Did you see that? He had taken the dragon and was using him to kill my family. We've gotten to this point before. In the past, we've tried to kill the man, but we failed."

"They were all dead, he ended our lives and.... How is it that we start over when all of us have died in the past?" Rider told her he didn't know, and tried not to think about what he'd seen before the knife had been taken from him. His mother's broken and burned body. Linyah, her belly still swollen with child, her head removed. His brothers' bodies too, Misha curled around his son, his body just as blackened as his father's. "Rider, we have to go back."

"I know." He didn't want to and he was pretty sure that she knew it. "I don't understand how that blade, here in the middle of nowhere, showed us that."

"Nic told me that we had to see that the man died." He looked up at Graham then. "When we were on the deck and you left, Nic came to me. He told me that should we not come together all will suffer. That without us, no one lives. Not any of us. He said again, like he knew that we were going to do this again."

"Why not? I mean, what is it about my family that everyone living seems to hinge on?" She laid her head on his chest and Rider almost asked her not to tell him. "He told you."

"Nic said that at one time leopard shifters were considered the second hand to many kings and queens. They could and did go into homes and kill their enemies, stealing plans for attacks, or whatever was needed of them. Even the dragon wasn't as feared as the cat shifter was. And because of their coloring, leopards could stand and wait in the darkest of nights and never be seen." He told her that they weren't the dark leopard, but the lighter colored ones. "Yes. You were revered even more. The fact that you could hide in plain sight, in dark or day, made your kind the most feared of all."

"What does this have to do with Sonya and her hatred of us?" Graham sat up then, her legs on either side of his hips. Rocking upward, his cock at her apex, he watched need roll over her as she sat there. "If you don't want this, then I would suggest that you move now. For as much as I need answers, I need you even more."

"Let me finish first." He tried not to think of her finishing and what that might mean to him, so he put his hands on her hips and held her still. "Sonya wanted to be queen, as you know. And she had enlisted the help of a leopard to come advise her. She knew that the current queen had no such advisors, and thought that it would be easy for her to take over with one. Then the cat turned on her."

"In what way?" Graham moved, rolling her hips over his cock until he was cross eyed with the need to plow her. "Tell me quickly."

"Your ancestors. The leopard that she had was one of your great too far back relatives that refused to help her. Rider, touch me, make me come." He touched his thumb to her clit, smelling her need, her wetness as he did so. "Yes, more. Give me more."

"Tell me first. Tell me how she thought he betrayed her." Rider was nearly ready to tell her to forget it, he was hurting now, his cock nearly ready to spill. But it was exciting too. Making her wait, having her keep on track when both of them were so needy. "Why did he refuse to help her?"

"He told her that the Lanning leopards were honest men. Worthy men that would never usurp a queen for the gain of one so cruel. You see, she'd killed his parents, murdered them both in their beds and took him away from them. The child, Rider James Patrick Lanning, was the one who thwarted her. Now fuck me."

He rolled her to her back, stripping her clothing off with the claws of his cat. When she was naked beneath him, Rider wasted no time in filling her. Slamming his cock deep within her, he loved it when she screamed out his name as she came. And when she commanded him again to give her his all, Rider leaned into her throat and bit her just as he came hard and quick.

CHAPTER 5

It wasn't enough, not nearly so. So when he continued to fuck her, drinking deeply from the wound he'd made at her throat, Graham jerked his head from her and looked at him.

"You belong to me now. And no other." He nodded as his cock moved in and out of her. Blood, her blood, dripped from his lips. "Come in me, Rider. I need to feel your cum fill my body again."

She wrapped her legs up over his and dug her heels into his muscles. Rider looked down at her, his face part cat and part man, and told her that he was hers. Even as he pulled her tighter, cupping her ass and making each of his strokes deeper, harder into her, she knew that he was being careful of her. That he was giving her as much pleasure as he could before he took his own.

Her need to touch him, mark him, had her fingers dancing over his hard flesh. Muscles filled her hands, sweat made them slide over his skin easier. Even as he fucked her, taking her to heights she knew that only he would ever give her, she held back some of herself. Not from him, never that, but for that final plunge, the time when he marked her as his own and she him. And when he paused, even his heart seeming to skip a beat, Graham pulled his wrist to her mouth and waited.

While he watched her, his body finally falling over the edge, she sank her teeth into his flesh and came with him. Their bodies, their hearts, were one in that very moment in time. And as he emptied in her twice more, bringing her over the edge so many more times that she lost count, he held her, being gentle with her. Finally, he cried out, biting her deeply again as he took her a final time over the edge of the cliff.

Rider dropped over her, his cock still thick and hard deep inside of her as he rolled to his back, taking her with him. Had there been a stampede coming at them, Graham was sure that they'd both be trampled by it, neither of them having the strength to move, much less take cover.

"I'm sorry." She lifted her head to look down at him when he spoke. "I wanted to give you so much pleasure that you'd think me a god. All I did was take. I'm sorry for that."

"Rider, I have no idea where that thought came from, but if you had been any more generous with your body, I might well have died here." She laid her head on his chest, feeling his soft chuckle. "Now lie still while I rest. I have a need to feel if you can live up to your name in a moment."

He rolled her to her back again and rocked into her. She wasn't sure she had it in her just yet to come again, but he didn't stop, didn't slow when she begged him again for a rest.

"I think I could fuck you right here for the rest of our days." His hips moved then, twisted enough that she cried out in pleasure. "Come for me baby. I want to see your face, see if your eyes darken more when you're coming."

His hands were at her ass, breasts, and throat. Even as he

fucked her, his body moving slowly in and out, he watched her. Images came to her then. Her leaning over a bed while he fucked her from behind. His cat with his tongue buried deep in her pussy as she screamed out a climax. The big cat chasing her down, nipping at her naked skin then fucking her again with his thick tongue. Holding onto Rider as he showed her all the things he wanted to do to her, she knew that when she came, she was going to be swallowed up in darkness.

"My cat wants to do all those things to you and more." Her pussy soaked, her breasts tightened at his words. "He would lap at you, touching his rough tongue to your pretty clit, his teeth scraping over your nether lips while he ate you. Can he, Graham? Can our cat have his piece of you as well?"

"Yes."

Even as she finished the word, he was shifting, his large cat moving down her body, his sharp teeth cutting into her flesh and then his tongue sealing the wounds. He was tasting her, she knew, getting her scent and flavor as he moved. And when he licked her pussy, his tongue deliciously entering her, Graham came hard, screaming her pleasure even as he held her down with his great paws.

After coming so many times that she'd lost count, Graham begged him to stop. To let her rest or die. Her body was spent, her heart pounding in her chest. And as the cat moved back, giving her a much needed breather, she felt the magic tighten around her and there was Rider.

His tongue was so different than his cat's that she came three more times. He fucked her with it, lapped at her until she was weak. And when he lifted her legs up to his shoulders, his cock filling her, she watched his face as he slid into her. Graham was pulled from the ground then and wrapped herself around him as he held her to him.

"You've nearly killed me." Graham laughed. There wasn't anything left in her, but she laughed at his comment. "I'm going to take you home, then I'm coming back for the—"

"No. I don't.... Please don't take me home. I want to be with you." He told her that he needed to get the van back soon. "I don't care. We can finish this up, talk and get to know each other a little bit while we do this. I'm not ready to go back yet."

"All right." He still held her, his body hard under her hands, her fingers finding more places to touch him. "Can we not talk about dragons and knives then? I need to process, and I can't with all this other shit going on in my head."

"I'd like that as well. Just two people getting to know each other while they shop." He asked about the knife. "There is no knife. As of right now, it's just us and the things we buy."

As soon as they tried to get dressed, she realized he'd torn her clothing from her in his haste, and she worried what they were going to do. But he simply said for her to think of what she wanted to wear, like it wasn't any big deal for them to be able to manufacture clothing for themselves. She supposed in a way it wasn't for him. Making their way back to the van where they'd left it, he asked her what she was.

"Wiccan. I might be considered a little more than that, perhaps a sorceress too, but I just go by Wiccan. My father is a master, but few people know that. He likes to keep things quiet about what we are. I think it stems from how he was sought out by Sonya." Rider drove them back this time, his driving almost bordering on cautious. "You have a lot of mix in you as well; you know that, don't you?"

"Yes. Linyah, as you know, gave me a lot. Nildale and Sina, they shared a great deal with us as a family when Thomas became their son-in-law. Over the years, I think we've made pacts with all sorts of creatures. Vamps, and a few I'm not sure what they were." She laughed with him. "But like you, I'm just saying I'm shifter, leopard."

They drove to the line of cars and pulled over when they could. It would be a nice walk, just the two of them, but they took the wagon this time as well. As they walked, hand in hand, he asked her about his ancestor, the first Rider Lanning.

"I don't know a great deal about him, other than what I told you." He nodded. "I guess we'll have to talk to Nic. He seems to know a lot more than what he shared with me."

"I would imagine that he knows a lot about a lot of things." He handed her a copper pot, and she could feel that it had been used to make shot gun pellets during the First World War. "Why can I do this now, do you suppose? Feel things and their history?"

"I could before you came into my life. Not to the extent that I can now, but it was there. Mostly just smaller objects, and the touch would have needed to be fresh." They avoided touching other people, she noticed, and thought that funny and sad in a way. "The next time we pass a food stall, we should get something to eat. I'm starving."

They paid for the little pot and the plastic bag of red handled cookie cutters too. There had been green ones as well, the paint on them too fresh to have been from the thirties, so they skipped buying those. Moving on, they purchased several more items; an egg beater that had a green handle, this one authentic; a basket that was used to collect eggs; and a collection of silverware that wasn't worth much on the whole, but Rider thought that there might be some matches to the things that Laci already had in the store.

The diner that they stopped at served good food, but she was pretty sure it was the company she was with that made it special. Rider was funny, smart, and kind. When the waitress messed up his order, he didn't complain but ate it. As they were leaving, he paid for dinner for the couple in the corner with two children. And as they made their way back to the hotel that he'd been staying at, he held her hand. Not in a possessive sort of way, but like he needed to. Then he asked her if she would stay with him in his room.

"I don't want to assume anything, not with you." She thought he was being a dick, but he smiled at her. "I'd like nothing more than to have you in my bed, your body wrapped around mine, but we don't know each other, and I think I'd very much like to get to know you."

"I'd like that as well." Nodding, he paid for two rooms and took her to hers. "Rider, we're going to have to talk about this sooner rather than later. Right?"

"Yes. I know that. But not tonight. Not today. I just want to feel like things are normal, like we're a couple that is making headway into a relationship, and the other things don't matter. Just for one day, today with you, I want to feel like a simple man on a simple date with a beautiful woman." She nodded to him, her heart too full to speak, and he pulled her to him and kissed her on the forehead. "Now. We'll have some dinner, then we'll have some fun. I don't know what, but if you're up for it, we'll go out."

"Yes. Yes, I'd like that very much." He grinned at her and she felt her heart take a quick leap. "Rider, where the hell have you been all my life?"

"Right here, waiting on you to find me."

~~~

Shadow cut into his steak and let the blood drain to his plate.

He wanted it rarer, nearly raw, but the establishment just didn't seem to get that. As soon as it touched his potato, he cut into it as well and let the fluffy white starch soak it up. It was going to be a fine meal.

It would be over soon. The Lannings would be dead this time. The dragon would go dormant again or he'd have to kill him, and Shadow would be rich. He knew about the magic that he was to collect; he'd had a connection to it since he'd been asked to help Sonya. It was going to be more than he could spend in all the rest of his days. And he planned to live a great many of them when this was done. Shadow also knew that Sonya was dead. Good riddance to her was his feeling on that score.

Sonya had been a sadist. More than that, she'd been a fool too. He'd tried to tell her several times over the decades that she should just kill them now and stop making games of things. Now, not only were they still alive and her dead, but everything that she'd worked for was gone as well. Her gifted magic to him was still there, of course. And it was just as strong as the day she'd given it to him. He remembered receiving it from her and the pain that had followed him for days after. As far as gifts went, it had been the worst he'd ever gotten.

The steak was juicy and tender, and he ate several bites of it before he ran two large bites full of his potato through the juices again. Bloody and raw. It was like he enjoyed a great many things in his life.

The man sitting across from him didn't speak. Neither did Shadow for that matter, but Shadow had a reason; Jim simply didn't like conversation. He'd talk if he had something to say, which wasn't often, but right now they were both content to eat and nothing more.

Shadow moved the salad that he'd not wanted out of his way

in favor of the rolls. There were a great many of them, soft and gooey, and slathered in butter. He glanced up at Jim when he set his fork down, knowing that he wasn't finished eating.

"There might be some issues with them Lannings that we gotta deal with." Shadow nodded. "They got security out the ass."

Again he nodded and pulled out his notepad to write his response. He wrote that he'd get around it when the dragon was freed. Nodding once, Jim went back to his meal.

Shadow and Jim had been partners for nearly a thousand years. Jim was human, or he had been, and Shadow was a dragon trainer. And not from this realm. When he'd come here, just after the dragons had been put to rest, he'd been left for dead with his throat cut. He'd not been as privy to the way things worked in this world, and had said the wrong thing to a bad man. But Jim had come along, picked him up, helped him heal, and had not left him since. He supposed in a way that Jim was his protector. And Shadow his.

Shadow hadn't been fired from his job for the king and queen. It had just finished and he'd become bored, and decided to come to this realm. In fact, they'd been very good to him. He'd been given a lovely home, payment for his services that would last his entire life, as well as a title. Dragon trainer had been a big deal all those years ago. Now it meant very little. And nothing here.

He knew that the dragons were all there. Put to sleep by him when the need for them was diminished. Now a few of them, the older ones, were free to roam the other realm. But it was the one that he'd taken with him that he knew was going to make him win this war.

"Your nose is bleeding again." Wiping his napkin over his face, he saw that there was more this time than before. Holding it there, he looked at Jim and saw that he was concerned. "The dragon, he's doing this."

He was. The dragon wanted out, freed. He'd been pissed off when put into Shadow all those centuries ago, and now that he knew that things were coming to an end, so to speak, Draconal fought him more and more every day, trying to be free of him forever. Especially since he'd seen the girl with the Lannings.

They finished up their meal and left. The magic that he used, it opened a great many doors for them both, as well as closed a few when that was necessary. Sonya had told him that he could use whatever she had whenever he wished, so long as he didn't hurt her. As they made their way to the truck, he paused when the dragon moved over his arm. He shouldn't have been able to do that.

"You okay?" Nodding then shaking his head, Jim only nodded. "Been thinking we need to get this done. You ain't well no more."

No, he wasn't. Something was different, and he didn't care for it. It had something to do with the woman getting to the Lannings before he got to her. As he sat in the truck, he closed his eyes and looked for her father. He'd be the key, Shadow knew this, but getting to him was proving to be a might difficult. Even when he'd seen him in his own home and around it, Shadow had been blocked somehow from touching him. Even reading his mind.

"Been thinking on things." He looked over at Jim to show him he was paying attention. "Do you suppose we could go and wake us up one of the other dragons and bring them here?"

Shaking his head no, he signed to him that it was no longer possible for him to go back and forth between the worlds. That was something else that had surprised him and pissed him off.

Someone had taken away his privileges.

He'd always had the ability to go home. And then for the last couple of weeks, not only couldn't he access the things he needed, like money and other items that had been given to him, but his money no longer appeared for him as his payment. Not that he really needed the money, that wasn't it. But he'd been promised it, and Shadow had worked hard for them. The very least they could have done was tell him what was going on. Or let him talk to them about it. He did wonder if they even knew it had stopped coming to him.

Pulling shadows around himself and Jim, they entered the hotel. The two of them had been staying here for a few weeks now, since they'd found that the last of the Lanning men was still without his mate. But almost as soon as they bypassed the front desk, someone called out their names.

"Mr. Shadow, I'm sorry to bother you, but there seems to be a problem with your room." Jim asked him what it might be. "Well, we don't seem to have a credit card on file for you. I know that you must have registered one when you checked in three weeks ago, but we've gone over our records several times and we just simply do not have one. If you'd be so kind as to take care of that now, we can get this cleared up."

Shadow felt confused. Which, he supposed, was a good way to feel when not only was the man right that they had checked in three weeks ago, but as far as anyone knew, they'd not been seen so hadn't bothered with any sort of check in service. He lifted his hand to use his magic, thinking, hoping really, that it had worn off, when he saw Nic standing behind the hotel manager.

Shadow assumed that Nic had taken care of it for them. And perhaps he was here to explain the glitch in the money situation, as well as his inability to go back and forth between realms. So when Nic followed them into the elevator, Shadow looked at the man and realized that he was armed more than he'd ever seen him, and that he wasn't talking. Shadow knew then that someone had figured out what he'd been doing here. And he thought, too, that he was in deep shit.

"You are, as a matter of fact. And nothing has been settled with the bill. I'm afraid that he's going to find you again and demand payment." Shadow leaned back against the wall as they rode up to his floor. He wasn't concerned. Something would happen, but he'd not be responsible for any of it. "Also, you will need to figure out other means of transportation. I've made sure that the limo company has realized that you have not given them any sort of payment."

Shadow was pissed, but tried his best to not look it. He loved riding in the big cars. Jim did as well. He'd never learned to drive, neither of them had. It had been too scary at first, and then later, laziness he supposed, had kept them from figuring it out. Besides, why drive when you could have your ass carted around all the time? He wondered why Nic would care if he took a few rides or not.

When they entered the room, there sat the queen, Kendra and her mate, the king, Tristin. Neither of them looked very happy to be there. Well, he wasn't either. And as he started to sign his questions about what had happened, Kendra cut him off.

"Hello, Shadow. We've heard about the unfortunate accident that has taken away your ability to speak. So for now, while we are here, you may speak. And before you do, know that you cannot lie to me or anyone in this room." She glanced at Tristin, and Shadow wondered what they were saying about him. "You've had all your weapons removed as of this moment as well. And Jim, your companion, will not help you in any way. If he does so, he will forfeit his life."

"Where is my money?" It felt strange to use vocal cords that had not been used in decades. His voice was harsh, sort of dry sounding, but she seemed to understand him. "And I'd like someone to explain to me why I can no longer go home."

"Money? Oh, the severance pay that you were to get once you left my services, is that what you're referring to? That has been revoked." He asked her why. "Not that I need to explain myself to you, but you violated your contract with us when you tried to have my sister killed. Not to mention, you've stolen something of great value from our realm."

"Nay, I did no such thing." An image of Linyah appeared before him, and he saw himself firing into a crowd that she was with. He'd known that she was there. He'd been ordered to kill her on sight. But there had been others there, too, that he'd been after. The fucking Lanning men. "So? I was following orders from Sonya. And what business does your sister have with the Lannings?"

"She is married to one of them. Thomas Lanning is her mate and my brother-in-law. Her family is now my own." Shadow felt his knees weaken a little, and he sat down in the chair when it hit him behind the legs. "You have tried to harm a member of the royal family, and you have used your magic for your own personal gain. Not to mention you have been killing people, others on a list that Sonya gave you, for no other reason than for yours and her personal gain. What do you have to say for yourself?"

He felt trapped. No, not trapped...like he was already in a cell and being tortured. He didn't care for that feeling. This wasn't his fault, his mind screamed at him, but that of Sonya. It came back to her being a cruel monster. So instead of trying to get out of his mess, he thought to anger the queen enough to take him to a cell. Once there, he knew that he'd be well fed and cared for. Perhaps enough to have the dragon removed safely.

"How am I to live without funds? Where am I to live, have transportation and other necessities? You've taken and taken from me, and left me with nothing to even care for myself." Kendra said nothing. "You made me a promise and now you have backed out of the deal we have made. What do you have to say for yourself?"

He'd done it. Made her so pissed that she was going to take him away. Shadow knew it the moment that someone wrapped their arm around his neck and lifted him from the chair. It was Nic; the smell of death seemed to stink up the air around him wherever he went.

"You cannot kill him, Nic. Not yet." He was let go. but not gently. As Shadow picked himself up from the floor, he decided that he could make a better impression standing. Tristin laughed and Shadow wanted to tear his throat out. Kendra must have felt his anger at the man or his intent, because when he made to lunge at her mate, she stopped him cold with just her voice. "Touch him and you will never feel your heart beat again."

He didn't want to die. Not here on this realm. He knew that death would eventually come for him; he'd broken the law of their land. But he also knew that if he stayed here the dragon would burn him up. Kill him in ways that would make him suffer. Shadow, all of a sudden, had had enough of this shit. But he still needed to get home, however he could.

"Why are you here? Was it only to tell me why I'm no longer being paid? I don't believe that. You have lesser beings that you could have do that for you. Is it to tell me to back off? I won't. So you might as well kill me now. Or have your brother do your dirty work." He laughed; it was forced, even he could hear it. She had taken a great deal from him, but he wanted more. When she stood up, he didn't bother backing away, nor did he lower himself before her. "I don't recognize you as my queen. I haven't for a very long time."

"Then you will not miss what you have been given."

The snap of her fingers brought him to the floor. His nose started to bleed profusely, his body hurt in places that hadn't in a very long while. The dragon moved over his skin, and Shadow was afraid to see if he was tearing at him, opening wounds that he knew would never heal now. When he sat up, his head light and his belly sick, the king and queen were gone and there was only Nic.

"I could kill you now. I'm not permitted, but I could do it so easily." Shadow asked him what was stopping him. As much pain as he was in, he'd almost relish it. "You have a destiny. And while I could care less what you think you must do, the way your life is ended will be justice for us."

"What if I told you that I no longer care to play in Sonya's game? That I only wish to end everything?" Nic said that he didn't really care, that it was much too late now anyway. "Nay, I don't believe that. There is always a way. I wish for you to take me in, put me in irons, in a cell so far below the earth that the sun will never touch me again."

"No, I will not. It is written that you will try and end the Lanning family. Try or not, I don't care. But it is written that you will try." Nic stood up and Shadow felt the wound at his throat, the pain fresh feeling after all this time, and put his hand to his neck. "You were only allowed to speak to us because she wanted it so. Now that she has left you, you'll find that a great many things that you had before are no longer yours to keep."

He held his neck, fearful of his head falling off. Looking for his man, he saw Jim standing still, as if he were encased in stone. When the shoes appeared in his vision, he spit on them and felt anger when Nic laughed. Then, like the queen, he was gone.

Oh, and the dragon? You will learn soon enough what it is to have captured something as grand as him. I shall enjoy watching the Lannings take you down. Nic's laughter pissed him off, so much so that he tried to roar with it. But all it did was hurt him, and Shadow let the pain and darkness that accompanied it take him under.

Chapter 6

Graham found her dad in the backyard, digging in the dirt, pulling weeds and putting other items in a large basket. He'd been carrying that thing around since she'd been only a child. Sitting beside him and pulling weeds with him, she wondered how to begin to tell him what she knew.

"When was the last time I was able to do this? Sit out in my yard, deal with all manner of weeds and small bugs and such. Long time. Very long." She nodded and asked him what he was going to do with what he had. "That mate of yours, he's given me permission to have me a building. Even had a crew come out and ask me what I wanted. I'm telling you, if he wasn't your mate, I might take him for my own."

They both laughed. Her dad was happy and she was so glad for that. "Dad, we've decided to be together."

"Didn't know there was any choice in the matter. Honey, don't pull the tansy up just yet. I want it to mature."

She left the weed looking item in the dirt as she moved around to the wild mint. "I don't guess there is, but we're dating.

Sort of being like a regular couple."

He stared at her for several seconds and she felt her face heat up. "Regular couple, huh? How do you think that is going to work when you're a Wiccan with powers out the yin-yang, and he's a hyped up leopard that can tear into a man with one bite?"

Okay, there was all that to deal with. Just last night when they'd been having sex, the entire bed had lifted from the floor and then dropped down as soon as she released. Rider had been so pleased with the action that he'd tried nearly all the rest of the night to make it happen again. The man was a dork. Graham noticed her dad looking at her oddly.

"What I mean is, we're going to not just be all over each other all the time. We're going to go out to dinner. See a movie and try to like each other first." Dad just shook his head and said nothing as he pulled out a few more weeds "He and I had separate rooms at the hotel. And then he took me to dinner at a really nice place."

"How much time did you spend in this separate room? Did you even get the bed messy?" She was really glad that he wasn't looking at her. Her face felt on fire now. "I'm thinking that you and him, you're going to do what is necessary to make you feel good, but it all comes down to being mates. He's a leopard, like I said, but he's more than that. You know that, right?"

"Yes. He showed me some of his magic." She glanced at the sigil on her arm. "This has happened before. All of this killing and the dragon and the man. Did you know that?"

"Yeah, Nic came by and told me all about how each time the Lannings fail, then it starts up again almost immediately. I asked him how that worked, and he said that nature kept the line going and he wasn't sure how. I don't think we wanna know, if you want the truth of it. He didn't mention if I died, but I'm assuming that I do." Her dad looked at her as he continued. "Did you know that at one time Nic and his family were the most powerful beings in any realm? Hell girl, any worlds."

"Yes. I knew that." She pulled a few more weeds then simply stuck her hand in the soil and closed her eyes. As soon as the earth granted her permission to help the soil along, she made the herbs that her father used all the time grow faster. He just laughed again. "Dad, I'm trying to talk to you. Can you pay attention for a moment?"

"Yes." He put his trowel down, as well as his trimmers. When he looked at her, she could see that not only was her father happier than she ever remembered him being, but he looked healthier as well. "Getting out and about, it's helped me in ways you can't believe. I'm sleeping much better, and longer too. I get to feel the sun on my face whenever the mood strikes me. And I have good conversations with people that I like. Nildale comes by. Nic and Kendra, as well. Did you know that she's not just the queen of her realm, but holds a couple of offices here too? Just to watch over people she sent here. And then there is Rider. Better man than him, I'd not know it. He's kind, smart, and he's got this way about him that just makes you feel calm. I know you can see it; I can too when I see myself. And Laci, she gave my mirror back too. Feel good about seeing my old friends and all."

"The man that's coming here, his name is Shadow." Dad nodded, then looked shocked. "Yes. I knew that you'd remember him. He's the one that has the dragon too, I'm afraid."

"Do the rest of them know?" She said that they didn't yet, but she'd tell them soon. "It had better be soon, love. If he comes here, he's going to be hard to deal with. Holy moly. Shadow is back, is he?"

"Nic told me that he and his sister went to talk to him, and they took some of his magic away. They couldn't take it all because of the dragon. It would have harmed the dragon should they have done that." He nodded. "But I don't know what to think now that we're marked too."

"Marked?" She showed him her sigil. "Rider, he has one too? About the same place? You know what this means, don't you? About the mark?"

"To be honest, no. I thought it was because we were going to have to free it, but it moves." She pulled her sleeve up more and watched as the dragon seemingly took flight and flew up her arm to her elbow. "He moves all over my body. Last night he was on my foot and I wasn't able to put my shoes on. It was kind of scary."

"You can control him." Graham shook her head. "You can. I'm not sure how that works just now, but I'm betting we can figure it out. You think you can summon him to you? By the way, I'd not do that just yet. We don't know what size he is. Could be that you can simply let him live on you.... No, won't work either. He has to feed. I'm wondering if he is feeding off Shadow. That'll make him right weak."

Her dad was thinking. He would throw out ideas then dismiss them almost as quickly. As he went over a list of possible things she could do with the mark, she thought of what else she'd been able to do since Rider had come into her life.

Things spoke to her, stronger than they had when they'd been antique shopping. Not just items that had no voice, but everything, including animals and plants. Before him she'd been able to talk to wild things, such as hawks, and birds. On occasion she'd been able to have a short, but very unsatisfactory conversation, with a squirrel. But now all she had to do was touch something; it mattered little if it was manmade or not. She could understand the person who had made it, the strife and love that it might have been used for. And if it was something that had been used with violence, she felt that too.

"Let me think here." Her dad seemed to close down; she'd seen him do this before but it made her no less frightened at what he might see. "This dragon, can you see him? I mean in real life; can you see him skyward?"

"Once. Rider and I saw him together. In the field behind this house." He asked her if the dragon was there or that was where they'd seen him. "Both."

Her dad looked at her. She knew it was going to be bad, whatever he told her. And when he stood up, picking up his basket, she followed. Rider had said he'd be back soon, he had to drop off the things in the van that they'd gotten for the shops, then he'd return to her. But she wasn't sure she wanted to wait.

"I'm thinking this has something to do with why you're here." She wanted to ask him what, but he moved on before she could. "There are spells we can bring up. I know of one or two that will bring us a clear picture of what he might need from you, but then we might not really want to know that either."

"Is he here to kill us?" Dad said he didn't think so. He pulled out his leather bag and began pulling things from it. The thing looked to only be about ten by nine inches, but it was magical and held a great deal more than that. Even the book that he now had opened was nearly two by three feet, and weighed about ten pounds. Yet a person would never know that to see the bag. When he opened the book to some drawings, he asked her if the drawing that he had found on the page was her dragon. "Yes, that's him. But he has a scar on his left side, like he'd been spiked or something."

"Good to know. I would imagine that was how he was subdued. If this is your dragon...well, darling, we might have a little trouble here." She looked over his shoulder at the drawing. "That's him, right?"

"Yes." The drawing had been done by the previous owner of the book. Of course when her dad had gotten it, the book wasn't nearly as thick nor as wide. As she and her dad had added to it, the book had adjusted itself to accommodate the new information.

When she ran her finger over the drawing, the dragon pulled from the page and became as real as if he were sitting in front of her. Then he spread his wings for her, turning so that she could see all of him. He was a magnificent creature, she thought.

"The first of his kind, Draconal was born of the earth, wind, and fire. The sea contributed to his birth by giving him the ability to hide within the depths of water when needed. His blood runs through the cold veins of every dragon born. His strength is beyond measure. His intelligence is incalculable. He serves only one." Her dad looked at her when the dragon turned to face them. "Graham, look what he has in his hand."

CHAPTER 7

Rider tried to think what he was supposed to do now. As he stood in the kitchen, he looked at the mess on the table. He supposed it wasn't really a mess but a work area, so he wasn't sure what he was to do with it all. Just as he was thinking to leave it alone, Misha showed up. He was never so glad for someone to take his mind off something as he was right then.

"What is this?" He told him he thought it belonged to Allister. "And does he have a habit of leaving his things out like this?"

Misha picked up the very drawing that had scared Rider into not touching anything else. He'd looked at it for over five minutes, trying to decide if it was just something that Allister had doodled around with or someone had made a joke. He was hoping for either of those scenarios.

"It's a dragon." Misha nodded without taking his eyes off the paper. "I think it's a good drawing, don't you? I mean, I thought it would be very nice in the antique shop in a nice old frame. It would have to be a large one. Matted for the best look. The colors are nice too, and I love that it's a dragon. Dragons can be—"

85

"Rider." It was all it took to have him break down, Misha simply saying his name. "Do you have any idea what this is? And no more babbling."

"No." Misha nodded and laid the drawing back where it was. "I came in here to get an early start on my day. I know that Allister was up late, I heard him down here a couple of times. And Graham is still asleep. We've decided to sleep together. Well, sleep isn't all that plentiful. I'm in love with her and she is very beautiful. We've been making plans, she and—"

Misha said his name again. "Take a deep breath and let it out slowly. And while you're doing that, I want you to not think of this drawing or the leopard in his hand, all right?"

"Yes. All right." He did as he was told, his mind in overload with all the things he'd seen in the picture. "Did you look at it? I mean, really look at the drawing, Misha. There are other creatures there. Ones that make up the dragon."

"I saw them." Rider nodded and inhaled through his nose and let it out of his mouth slowly. "Have you tried to contact anyone?"

"No. I wasn't sure what to say to them." Breathe, his head told him. Just breathe. "There are unicorns and gnomes in that dragon. Did you see them?"

"Yes. I did. I want you to reach out to Graham or her father. Tell them to come to you." Rider nodded, but didn't do as he'd been told. "I'm going to hit you if you don't fucking help me here. I'm freaking out too."

He reached for Allister and was surprised at the ease with which he was able to do so. Almost as soon as he touched the man's mind, he was in the kitchen with them. Both he and Misha jumped back from him when he started talking about.... Well, Rider wasn't sure what he was talking about.

"There are so many variables that I just simply had to step back from them. Then there was the way that I kept working on the circle. It's not, by the way…a circle, I mean. Also, you should know that the garden out back, it has nearly all the things that I need, and lucky for me there is a lovely shop in town that has the rest. I should have thought of that when we left the other time, but then there wasn't much in the way of time." Rider looked at Misha and wondered if he was getting any of this. He didn't seem to be. "I have a list of things you have to do. I think you can talk to him."

"Him?" Allister smiled and nodded at him. "I don't…. Do you mean the man that is trying to kill us?"

"Oh no. That wouldn't do any good, do you think? No, no, that's not who. The dragon." Rider sat down, his legs just going out from under him. "There is a way to do it. You would have to work with my Graham on it. I suppose that she's your Graham now. No matter, but you should really consider it."

"Talk to a dragon. Oh sure. And when he's eaten me, or burned me to a crispy fry, do you suppose he'll have anything to add to this madness?" Allister asked him why he thought he would burn him. "Because he's a fucking dragon."

"I don't think you're understanding me very well. I should have explained it better. Sometimes when I'm excited, my mouth and mind are not on the same wave length. Could be because…. Well, never mind about that. No, the dragon won't burn you, my dear boy. He belongs to you. Serves you, so to speak." Rider wasn't sure what to say so he said nothing. "You see, since you connected with him, he's been working to get free to come to you and Graham."

"How did we connect with him? And why do you think we'd want to?" Allister explained that he was given the connection and he shared it with Graham. "So I had this connection with him and since we're mates, it has gone to her as well. I guess that would—"

"You had him there all along. I would imagine that you were given him when you were touched by Linyah, but then I'm not sure about that. Regardless, you have it. If it was her, then Linyah gave you the power to connect with a great many things. From the beginning, I would imagine. But since he's been...well, I would say since he's been attached to that unsavory man, you've had some difficulties reaching him. But with the boost of power from Graham, you are both stronger."

Rider was trying to sort things out in his head. There was just too much, so he reached for Linyah. She told him she was a little busy but would get back to him soon. Graham joined them in the kitchen seconds later.

"I was just explaining to Rider about the dragon." She looked at him and he knew that she'd heard about him before this. "The connection you have will be stronger now, enough so that you could possibly bring him here."

"Now?" Rider looked at Misha. He sounded panicky, like he was terrified that there was a chance that the dragon could land in the yard at any minute. "We need to slow down, regroup, and talk about this in a timely manner, and not this jumping around thing. You've gone from gardens to shops all the way around to Linyah and Rider. I just need some order, timelines, and what we're going to do."

"All right, I can do that. But perhaps it would be easier if all parties were present. Such as the family. I'm afraid that this will affect them as well." Misha asked him how. "They will need to help Rider and Graham when the dragon is freed. Love; he'll need the love of this family to feel calm."

~~~

Graham was sort of worried about Rider. He'd been sitting on the deck, just staring at nothing, for the last two hours. She'd even gone out to talk to him twice and he just sat there, holding his bottle of water without drinking from it. She was pretty sure that he had completely forgotten that he had it. When someone spoke behind her, she turned to look at Linyah.

"I came as soon as I could. I've been trying to help out with some things on my realm that my sister needed." She sat in the chair and rubbed her growing belly. "I never knew that one little creature could absorb so much of your energy. All I wish to do is nap or go to bed."

"It's a girl. I'm sure you know that, but it's not just the babe that is taking from you, but her magic as well. I think you're in for a handful with her." Linyah nodded, grinning from ear to ear. "I see. You know this."

"Yes. I can talk with her as well. Not like a person would to another, but we communicate. I'm very excited to see her in four weeks, three days, and eleven hours." Graham laughed. It was the first one in hours. "Rider needed me."

"Yes. He found out about the dragon today that you gave him." Linyah asked her what she meant. "Draconal? My dad thinks you gave him to Rider when you gave him magic."

"Draconal is the king of dragons. I could no more give him away than I could my father. And believe me, there are times when I wish that was possible. But Draconal is.... He's the dragon that the man has? The one that Nic spoke to yesterday?" Graham nodded, confused now. "I never gave him Draconal. I know the dragon — he and I worked together for a great many years — but I cannot give him to anyone."

"Then how did he become attached to Rider, and now me?"

Linyah said she had no idea. "We can see him. Rider and I, we can see him there, but.... My father seems to think that we can talk to him. In fact, he thinks it would be a good thing."

"If he's with the man—Shadow, Nic said his name was. If he's with him, then he's holding him with magic. And I would imagine that Sonya had a part in that as well." Graham said she had no idea. "If you can talk to him, and I have no doubt that the two of you can, you can ask him who helped him be captured and why."

"I don't think that's a good idea." Rider looked beaten, exhausted, and determined when he spoke from the doorway. "What if it's a trick of Sonya's and she has set us up for this? I'm not going to take any chances on harming those that I love."

"She might not have. What would be the harm in asking the dragon?" Rider started pulling things from the cabinets and fridge without answering her. "Rider, we might not have a choice in the matter. He needs our help."

"There are always choices. We may not like them, nor do we always pick the right one, but on this, I won't do it. It's too much of a risk. And when this guy gets here, if he comes, we'll deal with him just as we do everything else. As a family. Are you staying for dinner, Linyah?" He acted as if it was finished, going on to something else after he'd laid down the law. Graham looked at Linyah when she simply laughed.

"I'm not going to get in the middle of this. I have enough shit going on as it is." Linyah stood up then and stretched. "I won't be staying for dinner tonight. I'm afraid that Misha has decided that as a family we're going to discuss what you're going to say to the dragon when you talk to him. I'm pretty sure, to him, it's a done deal." After she bowed to them both, she was gone.

As Rider puttered around the kitchen, Graham tried her best

to get a hold on her temper. He did not just make a decision for them both without talking it over with her, and then act as if his word was law. When he turned and asked her if she wanted a baked potato, she did the only thing she could think of and punched him in the face.

When he fell to the floor she wanted him to get up so that she could hit him again. Her anger was so out of control for the problem at hand, she was frightened by it. But she wanted him to get up, to let her hit him again and again.

"What the fuck was that for?" She found that she wanted to hit him again and had to take a step back. "What is wrong with you? That fucking hurt."

"Good." Her body vibrated with the pain of fighting the need not to hurt him again. So much so that she had to leave or tear his head off, the power of her anger was so strong. "I'm leaving."

Never prone to violence, her actions made her sick to her stomach. And when she ended up in the large antique store, she hid herself among the shadows until she could get a better grip on herself. Graham had no idea what had made her that angry.

"You should know that even though I can't see you, I can almost taste the pain that you're in." Graham looked at Nildale, a man that she was as much terrified of as she liked. "Thank you. I like you very much as well. Shall we speak like this or would you like to join me in my offices?"

"I hurt Rider. I mean, I really hurt him, both physically and mentally. And I have no idea why, but I want to do it again." He nodded and she found herself in a beautiful room. "Where have you taken me?"

"My offices. You may leave when you wish, but I thought under the circumstances you'd be freer to speak here." He handed her a cup of tea and a small plate of cookies. "I have an idea what has upset you, but perhaps you should tell me. I'm a good listener."

"I hit him. Rider. I just punched him in the face as hard as I could and wanted to do more." Nildale asked her if she'd been provoked by him. "Yes. He decided, without asking me, that we were going to do things his way. I think there should have been at least a little discussion, don't you think?"

"Perhaps. But then you don't know Rider as we do. He's been the family worrier for some time. And rightly so. He and his brothers, they've gone through a great deal in the little time that I've been with the family. I would imagine that with the job that they did prior to this, their father, and them getting hurt a great deal, he feels he has good cause to be worried." She said that she wanted to hurt him more. "Yes. I understand that too, but we'll get to that in a moment. What is it you think to get from doing things your way? And I have taken a little peek at your mind. I know of the dragon and Rider's hold on him."

"Linyah didn't give him to Rider." Nildale said he didn't think she was able to do that anyway. "That's what she said. So how did he get picked to carry this dragon around?"

"I don't know that either. I'm having it looked into." She wasn't sure what that meant, but didn't care so long as there were answers. "You're going to have to talk to Rider. I believe he is trying to contact you."

"Not just yet. What did you mean when you said you'd get to it in a moment? I'd like to know why after all this time, I want to physically hurt someone that I love." Nildale smiled at her. "You might want to answer. Right now you're creeping up on my list of people to hurt."

"When Linyah first came to the Lannings, she offered first Hannah, then the rest, some of her power. I think she might have shared with young Phillip, but that was a necessity and not...never mind. She shared some of her power with the entire family, including your mate." Graham asked what sort of power. "Everything. Not in large doses, as she has it, but enough to keep them safe and the ability to communicate with them. We all have that."

"And she didn't give him the dragon then?" Nildale shook his head no and ate a cookie while she let her thoughts wander. "You're trying to tell me something and I'm not getting it."

"I would imagine that you would eventually, but since we're pressed for time, I'll tell you. Linyah took Rider as her own. As in, he was in her keeping. She told me that she didn't know why she'd been told by her brother to do that, and still doesn't. But Nic did tell her that she needed to protect him above all others, and so she has." Graham asked him about Thomas, Linyah's mate. "Oh, he got the power along with the rest of the family when she shared. But Rider got more...he cannot be killed. Not by blade or magic, nor by anything that would normally kill us. And while it's not easy to kill us, nearly impossible without the right land, blade, and other factors, Rider cannot be killed by any means. And he doesn't fully belong to anyone but my daughter. And sadly, right now, that would not include you."

"Are you saying that while I love him with all that I am, he isn't mine fully?" He nodded again. Graham felt the pain of that all over her body. She thought that her heart even skipped a few beats because of it. "So Rider belongs to Linyah and that is why I'm so pissed at him. I'm assuming that it's not physical, nor is it that she loves him. Linyah is just protecting him. For me?"

"Some, but not all. I think it was her duty, after a time, to make sure that all the Lannings were safe. Rider was held for something special. For something; now we know that it has to do with the dragon." She asked him if he thought it was only the dragon. "I didn't know before, but I think someone else, your father, was protecting you for Rider. Am I right?"

Graham nodded. "He told me that he saw us together in the future. And that.... Did anyone tell you about the knife that we found?" He said that no one had, no. "We were doing that antique thing, he and I. Just getting to know each other, when we entered this stall. The blade was just lying there, and when Rider picked it up, it was as if we'd been transported through this sort of time warp and we could see them all. The entire family was dead. Even Linyah and her unborn child."

"Did the blade belong to the two of you, or the man who killed the family?" She told him she didn't know, but he used it against them. "And where is this blade now? I'm assuming that you've taken care that it's safe?"

"Yes. It's here. In this castle." Nildale grinned at her, nodding his pleasure at holding something so dangerous. "We thought that if no one could find it, then no one could use it against us. I hope that's all right."

"Yes. It's a splendid idea. I think perhaps it's the best place for it under the circumstances. Shadow can no longer return here, so he'd not get it, and no one but the three of us know that it's here." She told him that had been the plan. "Now, why you're so angry with Rider. It's because even though you're not a cat, you know that someone has been touching him. Metaphorically anyway. Once the hold on him is gone, you'll be just fine."

"And now what?" She turned to find not only Rider in the room with them, but also Kendra. He must have gone for her when she didn't answer him. "And why is it that you have my wife here?"

"We were discussing her need to harm you." Rider looked at

her as Nildale continued. "I believe that it's because of the hold that Linyah has on you. Could be, and this is just a guess on my part, that this is making Graham second in your life."

"She's not." Graham moved over when Rider joined her on the small couch. "I love her with all that I am, and would die for her."

"As it should be." Nildale stood up and nodded to Kendra. "Could you please have the Lannings brought here, my child? I think it's well past time that we have Linyah finish her duty for this young man."

Graham wasn't sure that this was the time or place for it, but had no say in the matter. Not when almost as soon as Nildale finished speaking they were all there. Even the children. As they were brought up to speed on what was going on, Rider told Graham how sorry he was.

"I had no idea that a decision that I made out of fear would hurt you so much. I shouldn't have been so upset with you. You have been dealing with this longer than I have. So I've been thinking, I believe that we will have to talk to the dragon after all. To leave him stuck there under Sonya's spell isn't right. If we can help him, all of us, we need to do it. It's the right thing to do." She nodded and laid her head on his shoulder. "I'm sorry about all of this, Graham. I had no idea what this magic would do to you."

"I'm sorry too. I should have been a little more understanding." He kissed her then, stopping her from saying much more. She looked up at him when he lifted his head. "Rider, what did I do to have someone as wonderful as you in my life?"

"I'm the lucky one."

They looked around the room when Nildale called things to order. Whatever happened now, it was going to be epic, and not at all a quiet discussion. Graham had to laugh a little. This family did nothing by half measures.

When Linyah stood up and turned to them both, she felt her anger soar up nearly out of control again. Calming it was a lot easier than it had been before. She was pretty sure that the woman standing in front of them was the reason.

"First of all, I need to give up my rights to Rider." When she winked at her, Graham had the most incredible urge to hug her for her understanding. "I should have done this sooner, and if you want to hug me after then I'm all for it. Right now I'd be afraid that you'd put a knife in my back." When she laughed, Graham changed her mind. She wanted to hurt her.

"I really hate that you can read my mind. When will I get to do that?" Rider cleared his throat and told her she'd had the ability the moment she became his mate. "I'm guessing that this has been asked before, but I don't suppose there is a book on all this stuff. And why can't I read your mind, Linyah? Is it something we can fix?"

"No, there is no fix. I'm sort of glad that there isn't. You can't read my mind because I gave the ability to Rider. You cannot read the one that shared. I never thought of you not being able to read mine too, but I think I like that idea. For now. But I do need to take my hold off him." Rider asked what would happen to him now. "Nothing will change. You're still an immortal, but instead of me helping you stay alive, Graham will."

"But I don't know what it is I'm supposed to do." Linyah said that her love would be more than enough. "That's sort of sappy, don't you think?"

Everyone laughed and she felt slightly stupid. But before she could snap at them, the urge still there to cause harm, Rider took her hand in his and kissed the back of it. And just like that, she felt much better.

"It's gonna hurt, I'm not going to sugar coat this."

And before Graham could say a word, Linyah took her other hand into hers and everything just simply blinked out. The pain she was in for that split second before passing out was incredible.

Chapter 8

Shadow looked out of the broken window of his new home. It was a far cry from where he'd been staying the last few hundred years. Mostly the places had been beautiful hotel rooms that would cost more in one day than some people made in a week. Other times it had been homes of someone that had simply left because he'd made them. He'd been taken care of by the most professional staff, and had clean bed linens and towels whenever he wanted them. But all that had come to an end. Without money or much magic, he had been reduced to living in the streets...or in this case, in abandoned buildings.

As soon as you're all dead, things will change, Shadow thought with a vengeance. He moved away from the window and decided that the view wasn't much better inside his hovel. He'd cleaned it up some; not much could help the place other than a heavy crane with a ball attached to it, but he and Jim had done the best they could. He sat on the large wire roll and thought about the man, Nic.

He'd not killed him. It had taken him nearly a day and a half to realize that not only should he have, but Shadow had given him every opportunity, not only by his actions during the time in the hotel room, but past ones as well. Shadow was alive, yes, but the fact that he really shouldn't be after encountering not just the big man, but the king and queen too, had left him a little curious. They'd not ordered his death, nor had they taken him away to prison as he had wanted. Why?

He thought it had something to do with the dragon he'd stolen, but wasn't sure anymore. Looking at the encircled beast, he was still amazed that he had him there. Not that he'd had much say in what had transpired that day. Sonya's chemist had told him what to do, and he'd done it. Shadow was just thrilled beyond words that he'd not died, as they had told him he might. He remembered Sonya taking him into the deep cave and telling him what was going to happen. Not all of it…had she done that then he wouldn't have agreed. At least he told himself that now. Back then, he might have agreed to a lot more things. Shadow had been stupid.

"I have such plans for you, Shadow. I think you, above all others I have working for me, are going to get the job done. And when I'm sitting on the throne in the big castle, it'll be you that's going to be sitting at my feet. This is my plan. You're going to steal the dragon. The big one." Shadow had told her that it wasn't possible for him to do that. "But it is. Just lure him to the area where I tell you, and once he's there, I'll make sure you have all the help you need when the time comes to kill those people. Kendra, the upstart, will be so heartbroken that she'll do just what she should, step down from her position and offer me the throne. I should have had it all along, but she'll come to her senses soon enough. But the best part will be that Linyah is dead."

He'd figured out a great many things about Sonya, but he

never understood her hatred for Linyah. Shadow had liked the beautiful warrior, even enjoyed her company when she'd come to the fields where he'd worked the dragons. Even Draconal had been easier to handle when she was there.

"Once you get him to the appointed field, I have a sorcerer that will come and help you take care of him." Shadow had asked her for what. "The two of you together are going to bring me the Lannings on a plate, and Kendra will no longer be queen. And then you, my dear sir, will be right there with me. Oh, won't it be wonderful to live in the castle?"

"I suppose so. But how does that work? I don't even think these Lannings are aware of the queen and the other realm. And even if they were, the Lannings are nothing more than a family of shifters. Not even good ones." Sonya had told him it was in the future. "Then kill them off now. Why wait until the future before you end their line?"

"Because I have a plan." Another thing he'd added to his list of oddities about Sonya was that she never deviated from her plan. Even if she could see how foolhardy it was, she stuck to it until the very end. Which usually didn't take all that long. "Once they are all dead and Linyah is as well, her stupid sister Kendra will fall to her knees to beg me to take the kingdom from her. It will be my greatest victory, to take her mate from her and have her sister fail."

"Kendra's mate?" Sonya told him no…just that, no. "I don't understand. I'm not magical, not really, but it would seem to me if you wanted to end the Lannings in the future, then killing them now would do that for you."

"But you are not me and it won't work. Don't you think I've tried this before? Many times have I thought to have ended them only to have them come back, their line stronger than before. No, my way is the best, as usual, and you'll do as you're told." He had wondered about that statement, how she'd done it before and had over the years realized that there was some sort of magical ring around the Lannings and their mates. He'd killed them off several times, including Linyah, but each time he did, every time he had thought they were done for, here they would be again. Shadow wondered even now if they were meant to live and he wasn't playing his part well.

But once he'd gotten the big dragon to come with him, they'd set off for the field in the other realm. It wasn't exactly what he'd thought of when he'd been asked to come to the field. Shadow had thought it would have been an arena, a place that Draconal could show off some of his skills. But it had been just what she'd said, a field.

"You will have to be hidden away after today; your movements will be monitored now. I should have thought of that sooner. I'll make sure you will be able to come and go to my realm, but you'll not be as welcome as you have been." He told her that it wasn't a fair thing she was asking him to do. "Oh, I think you'll love it, Shadow. There will be riches beyond your very imagination. Women will fall at your feet, and you will have such great power, power like you've never even thought of as my king."

"Your king of what?" She told him of her plan. "You've said this before. How you're going to kill the Lannings in order to stop Linyah from finding her mate, and to get Kendra to leave the kingdom to you. I don't know if that'll work, Sonya. I've been thinking about what you're saying. You do realize that there are her parents, as well as Nic, who could take over the kingdom should Kendra not wish to have it."

"They'll have to fight me for it."

Shadow had wisely never brought up her plan again. Her thinking was out of whack as far as he could see, and her ideas that someone in their position would just let Sonya come in and destroy all that they'd built was off as well. He had told her several times that the dragons would never harm the royal family. Magic held them in check, more than either of them had, no matter who commanded them.

"He'll do as we tell him or he shall never be freed." He'd asked her free from what. "Not what, but who. He's going to be a part of your body."

"I don't think so." But before he could leave her, taking the dragon with him, a blade pierced his chest, coming from his back. He looked down at the silver blade covered in his own blood and then at Sonya. "You've killed me."

"Nay, I have only prepared you for the dragon." As he blacked out, either from blood loss or from pain, Shadow heard Draconal screaming, his thunderous roar making his head spin.

"Sir?" Shadow pulled himself from his memories to look at his friend. Jim had been out finding them a better place to live, as well as food. And as he was empty handed, he could only assume that he'd had no luck at either task. "They're all in town. The Lannings as well as the king and queen. They seem to be having a large party of sorts."

Shadow pulled out his pad of paper, and Jim came closer to him to read as he wrote.

Are there any wolves with them? He said that there were. *So they're being protected? We have to get that woman before we can get any of this to work. Graham is the key to getting us what we were promised.* He ended that statement with several dollar signs.

"I don't suppose you could walk away, could you?" He asked Jim why he'd do that. "Because the witch is dead. The magic is gone as well. You know that they'll have found the money too. There won't be any riches either because of that. And I've an idea that we're not going to get anything we were promised. No magic, no money, and we've already lost all that magic that kept us going. I don't think that Lady Sonya was right in the head."

Nodding, he wrote as Jim spoke. *No, she wasn't. But I can't continue to hold this monster within me. His anger is killing me, tearing me apart.* Jim nodded and sat on the room's only other seat, another wire holder. *What's wrong, Jim?*

"Nic, he didn't kill us." Shadow nodded. "Why not? I'm sure he had his reasons. And him telling us that we're going to die, that didn't set well with me. I know it didn't with you none either. I had it in my head we were going to be rich and live to be millions of years old. I was looking forward to spending my years with you. I don't think that's going to happen now, do you?"

Nic had told them that he had a destiny. And that his death, however that might happen, would be justice for them all. How is that possible? he wondered. Not only that, but once he had the woman with him, how would they defeat them when the dragon was freed? Nic had sounded as if the dragon would matter little to the fight.

"That witch, do you think she had any idea that these men would keep finding their mates despite what she told us? I mean, so far even that one that was supposed to die by his own hand has his. And that sister to the queen, the one she told us was the key to whatever she had in her sick mind, she's fat with a baby. What do we got? Nothing at all." Shadow had no choice but to agree with his friend on that score. Everything they'd had was now gone. "I'm thinking that this is the end of us, Shadow. And no matter what happens now, this one, this time will be the end of us for good."

Shadow picked up the pad again to ask him what that meant, but Jim took it from him. There was a look in his eyes, one that said he was disappointed in him. Shadow stood up and put his hand over the knife at his side, only to come up empty handed. He wasn't sure what he might have done with the knife, but the need to have it was making him dizzy.

"You gonna kill me?" Shadow said nothing, frankly because he had no idea what he'd been planning or if he had been planning anything at all. "You're gonna have to. You know as well as me that it's the only way I can have peace. And you either do it right now or I'm going to try and kill you so that you gots no choice in the matter. I'd rather die by your hand than anything that has happened to me before with this stuff."

The knife was shoved into his hand. It was take it or be hurt by it when it fell to the floor. Holding the knife in his fist, Shadow tried to make his friend, his only friend, understand that he'd not be able to do this. What would he do without him? He was all he had in the entire world right now, either world.

"I'm dying. I done went and saw that clinic doctor whilst I was out. He said I'm done for. No curing me in time for you to get that magic you been promised, even if it was out there for us to be getting. End me now, Shadow. I don't want to suffer no more. I already hurt too bad to breathe around it. Please? You owe me that much." Shadow shook his head. "I can't do it on my own. I just can't. I tried, but I need to be gone before the suffering gets worse, and we both know it will."

The knife was turned in Shadow's hand, the tip of it touching the shirt of the other man. It was all he could do not to pull away and leave. But Jim told him again how much he didn't want to suffer.

It went into his chest surprisingly easy. He knew that Jim

worked hard to keep his tools cleaned and well maintained. His foresight on this, his need to have everything they had in perfect working order, had saved Shadow countless times, and now made short work of ending the life of the only man he'd ever trusted. As the life went out of Jim's eyes, his grip on Shadow lessened too, and Shadow felt like he was dying with him. He had to help Jim to the floor when he knew that he was close to taking his last breath.

"Thank you so much. You done good." Shadow wiped at the tears that blinded him to Jim. "I was set for a bad haul, I was. You saved me. But you gotta do me a favor now. You gotta run, Shadow. Run away now before it's too late. If'n it ain't already."

As he sat there, holding the knife in one hand, Jim's hand in the other, he thought about doing just what he'd been asked to do. Run. Not just from this, but he thought Jim was telling him to run from it all. He was going to be in for a bad haul himself before this was done, he just knew it.

~~~

Rider was overwhelmed. Not just that, but he wasn't eating or sleeping much. He smiled when he thought of some of the reasons he wasn't sleeping much and what the two of them, he and Graham, were doing instead of sleeping. That woman was the best thing that had ever happened to him.

Graham wasn't like the other women in the family. While they were headstrong, opinionated in a good way, and strong, Graham was that and so much more. She was confident in her decisions, and very creative when it came to sex.

"You all right?" He turned and looked at her, the water from the shower forgotten when she walked into the bathroom with him. "You've been in here a while and I thought you were hurt or something."

"Just thinking." He reached for her. "Why don't you join me and I'll wash your back? Then maybe I can get you to wash mine."

"I'd rather suck your cock." The bottle of shower gel in his hand squirted all over him and the wall beside him. "Oh look, Rider. You've used up all the soap. Whatever shall we do now?"

"You're trying to kill me, aren't you? I know it. It's your ploy to make me drained of everything I am by sex." She nodded, the grin on her face nearly taking him to his knees. "Well, I can't think of any better way to die than that. Come here."

She'd gotten the hang of stripping off her clothing by magic pretty quickly. He would find her in the oddest places, naked and ready for him. Twice he'd gone to the barn to get something for the house and had found her there, waiting for him. She'd either be holding onto one of the beams that held up the upper floors, or laying on a bale of hay with a blanket over it. When she entered the shower with him, Rider started to pull her to his body.

"Not yet. I need to touch you. I want to wipe my fingers all over your skin." He felt her breast touch his chest, her nipple scrape along his. "You're going to enjoy this."

The large sponge had been in the shower stall when he'd had the house decorated. He'd never used it, preferring not only a wash cloth to clean up but a bar of soap as well. The liquid soap had been Graham's addition to the bath. When she started to run the sponge over his body, Rider moaned in pleasure. It had been sexy enough watching her pour the creamy liquid over the thing, but as soon as it touched him, Rider knew a kind of pleasure he'd never known before.

"You have the most incredible skin. Soft and hard too. I love the way your muscles respond to my touch." She washed his arms, lifting them above her head and using the sponge gently over him. His fingers were washed as well, her fingers getting between his when the sponge wouldn't. "Turn around for me so I can wash your back."

He had to hold onto the wall. The way she rubbed his body down, the care she took to his spine, the sponge molding over his ass and shoulders, had his cock burning with need, his balls tight with fullness. He was stone hard, aching, but having the best time of his life.

Graham kissed his shoulder blade, bit gently at his ribs as she moved over him. By the time she had moved to his legs, he had to hold his cock or have it hurt more. As soon as she told him to turn so that she could wash the rest of him, he had to let out a long breath; the need to come all over her was so great. He turned and nearly whimpered.

Seeing her on her knees in front of him, her own need was there for him to see, almost touch, and he thought perhaps she was going to kill him. And when the sponge, a torture device he'd come to realize, moved over his cock, he nearly came when she cupped his balls in her hand.

"I want to taste you." He nodded, unsure if he could have spoken or not. "When you come down my throat, I want you not to hold back. I want all of you."

"I'm not going to last long. You've taken me as close to the edge as I could be right now." When she licked him from root to crown, he did cry out. "Christ, woman, finish me before I die here."

Her mouth seemed to engulf him to his very toes. She swallowed him past the tight muscles in her throat, and her hands held him while she rolled his balls around and around in her warm wet palm. Rider reached for her then, he needed to.... He wasn't sure what he needed, to hold on or to fuck her, but as soon as he touched the back of her head, she squeezed his balls tightly and that was all it took.

He came hard, his eyes rolled to the back of his head while she continued to bring him. And when she lifted her head from his cock, his cum still on her lips, Rider pulled her up to her feet when she licked it clean and smiled at him.

He needed to fuck her. Not make love…that would have been unsatisfactory to them both. But he wanted her under him, her pussy wrapped around his cock. Turning her so that her ass was at his groin, he bent her over the shower seat and slammed forward.

Rider had never been one to cause anyone pain, but he slapped her ass then, hard and without thought that he could have been hurting her. The second, then third time he hit her, making her ass a bright pink, he felt her tighten around him, her pussy nearly strangling him as she screamed out her release. But it wasn't enough. Not yet.

He lifted her from the seat and nearly tossed her onto the counter. Taking her again, fucking her in pounding, unrelenting strokes, Rider took her mouth. As she held onto his shoulders, her fingers digging deep into his flesh, he cupped her ass, bringing her even closer to him as he emptied into her once more. When she came with him, screaming out his name, Rider bit into her throat and tasted the hot spicy taste of her rich blood as he brought her over the edge again.

Graham came twice more as he fucked her. His body was spent, more than he thought it had ever been after sex. But as she relaxed in his arms, he felt badly for his treatment of her. Looking down at her, he was both startled and glad for the smile she gave him. Rider thought he could die right now as the happiest man in the world. Any world.

"If I come in here every day and give you a bath, will you end it like you did today?" He kissed her quickly, glad that he'd not upset her. "Rider, that was fucking fantastic. I meant for us to have some fun, but I have to tell you, that was.... Wow."

"It was my pleasure. I mean, really my pleasure. However, if you do that every day, I won't last a week. You've drained me." He backed from her slowly. "I hate to leave you today."

"I understand. And the rest of the family is coming over later anyway. I guess we're going to console ourselves by going shopping and doing some work around the shops. I heard Laci say that you had a fantastic week, and a lot of the things we picked up are gone already." He nodded, thinking that he'd rather stay behind too. "Does Misha think you guys will have any more luck than the police have?"

The call had come in an hour ago for them to be brought in, finally. They had been on standby, waiting for someone on that end to simply pick up the phone and invite them out for a week. There were three families missing, and no word as to when or how they'd disappeared. The local police were asking for help, but the Feds had said that they had it. So far they'd not *had* it very well. It had been nine days since the families had come up missing, and they all feared it was going to be a recovery rather than a rescue after all this time.

"We've been keeping in contact with the locals, and they're worried too. I guess this group went on a vacation every year together, and this year had been planned the same way. But the neighbors claimed that they were to leave on the tenth of this month. But on the ninth, all their houses were locked up, and the trailers that they'd planned to take were sitting in the driveways ready to go. In addition to not taking their very nice motor homes, their pets were left behind in the backyard."

That was what had alerted the first neighbor…the dogs in the back. She'd told Misha that their neighbors had loved those dogs like they did their family, and would never have left them out like that. Not in the rain and without food or water. After two days of no word, the police were finally left to calling in help. Unfortunately, the Feds they had called had no luck either. They were simply gone.

So today they were going to just go out there and lend a helping hand. Misha said he couldn't leave them without answers, and Rider and the rest of them had agreed. It was time to bring back Lanning Search and Rescue one more time.

"When you get back, Dad and I will have everything we need set up for us to talk to the dragon." He nodded as he moved about their bedroom, his mind on too many things at once to really concentrate on any one thing at the moment. "Rider, look at me."

He did, but knew when he saw the look in her eyes she was seeing everything. "I'm stressed out. Not about us, but about everything. I'd like to ask you a favor. Not a favor really, but for you to do something for us both. While I'm gone, I want you to think of somewhere we can go when this is done. I don't care where, or even if it's a lot of places. I'm thinking we need a month, more if you want. But a time to get away and be normal."

"I can do that." He watched her face, knowing that she was going to comment on the dragon and he didn't want to talk about it right now. "I love you, Rider. Very much so."

"I love you too." Rider pulled her into his arms and simply held her. "I'm going to be all right, but I've always worried overly about things. I need to let things go, but I'm not built that way."

"I understand." He nodded, but didn't let her go. "Also, your mom is going to be interviewing for cooks today and tomorrow. I think that'll take some of the pressure off us too. I'm sick of going out all the time."

It was a normal thing to be said. Rider felt like it was perfect for how he was feeling too. A cook. Someone to come into their home and do the mundane task of making them a meal. He thought perhaps it was the best news he'd had in some time. Lifting Graham's chin up so that he could look at her lovely face, Rider fell in love with her all over again.

He finished dressing and was in the kitchen when Misha showed up. He was late but he told Rider that the baby had spit up on his other shirt, and it had taken him longer than he'd thought to find another one.

"All my shirts are just not there anymore. And I've not purchased any either. I think I gave them away for rags or something." So had Rider. Not rags, but to be torn down for rag rugs for Ruby and the other women of the wolf pack. "On another note, did you hear anything back from the guy about the warehouse?"

"Yes, as a matter of fact I did. He's going to come out soon to see the area we're going to rent to him. I've talked to Mom about it, and she said that if he calls, she can direct him for us if we're gone too long." Rider still wasn't sure about that, renting rather than selling the property to the man. But the attorney had said it was a good investment and if he did fold, which wasn't going to happen, then they'd not be out anything but come out ahead on it. Mr. Knight was willing to put down a hefty deposit on the place that he'd forfeit if he bailed on them. "I have the information with me. I'll talk to you about it on the plane."

As soon as they were airborne, Misha asked him about it again. As Rider gave him the information, the others joined in. This was going to be a good thing, he thought. Jobs for the area, taxes for schools and other things, as well as money for them. He just hoped that this guy didn't back out as had happened before.

CHAPTER 9

The search was going longer than he thought it should. Misha looked at the map again and again, knowing that they were missing something. These people did not deviate when they had a plan, and had everything, including gas stops as well as restaurants and campground information, all detailed out. Even breaks for the drivers to get out of the motor homes to stretch and walk were on the list.

"The itinerary said that they were to leave at six in the morning from Amarillo and arrive in Dallas sometime after noon. There they would cook lunch, and rest up for two hours before moving on." Misha didn't bother turning to Rider when he spoke but nodded. "Then after that, they were set to drive for another six hours to get to Hot Springs, Arkansas. Where they would be staying for an entire day before moving on to Memphis, Tennessee to stop again."

"But they never left here." Rider asked him how they knew that. "We don't, not really. What we know for sure is that they loaded up the campers with enough food and gas for the start of the trip, and clothing for a two-week vacation. There is another list in each of the kitchens of things they were set to do the day before. Trash out, water turned off to the washer, toilets, as well as outside outlets. All things that had been done and marked off by someone in the household. There is also a mention of making sure that all credit cards were locked in safes in the campers. Which is done as well. All had their mail set to be stopped on the day they left and to be picked up by the homeowner the day after they returned."

"Okay. Cell phones have been pinged with no results. All of them were retired from their places of business, so there are no business credit cards to check from them, and the bank said that it was normal for them to take most of the cash from their accounts, but to leave some money until after they returned. Bills are paid up until next month. Taxes are paid as well. What the fuck, Misha. What are we missing here?"

"I have an idea." They both turned to Murph, who was looking worn out, more so than the rest of them because of the baby. "What if, and this is just a what if, they had been planning this for years? To just simply disappear. And over the course of the four years that they did go on vacations, they would sit around the campfire and plan the big escape."

"Really?" Murph stuck her tongue out at him. "First of all, to simply disappear like that would take more than just a little bit of planning over the course of a vacation."

"And? They didn't live far apart. We know that they talked a lot with each other. Perhaps they just got sick of living here and decided to leave." Neither he nor Rider said anything. "Look, it's believe that or aliens came here and took them away one night and are doing anal probes on them even as we speak."

"I think you need to take a nap." When she stood up to no

116

doubt hit Rider, the door to the room opened once again. Misha wasn't really surprised to see Nildale there, but he was to see four armed guards with him. "What's going on?"

"You're not going to like this, nor believe it either for that matter." Misha nodded but didn't say anything. "They aren't human."

"How do you...? Never mind. What are they?" Nildale said they were Doran. "You mean like Murph and her son?"

"Yes. They're not happy, you see, that they've been sent here with no means of support. They decided very early on that they'd not have children with such subhuman beings such as humans, and they planned to return to make their displeasure known." Misha asked if everyone was all right. "Yes. But...well, two of them are still missing. And we believe that they have plans to come after myself and my family."

"You think that they're here? On this realm?" Nildale told him that he knew that they were. "And by chance, do you know *where* they are on this realm?"

"Yes, they're here but for now, we can't find them. We're just not.... They'd taken precautions against us finding them." When he didn't say more, Misha felt his cat move along his skin. Wherever these people were, it was going to be bad. "I've taken it upon myself to have extra guards put around your families. Even Linyah has someone watching over her, as well as Kendra and Tristin."

"Should we leave here? Go home?" Misha thought they shouldn't have to ask, but Nildale was shaking his head at Rider. "Then what? We just sit here with our thumbs up our asses and —"

"Rider, sit down please." The calmness of Murph's voice startled him. When Rider sat down, Misha did as well. "Don't

117

move. I have an idea where they are. Just, please, don't move."

Max stood in the middle of the room then, just appearing next to his mom as if he'd been there all along. When the two of them joined hands and closed their eyes, Misha wished in that moment that he had someone to hold too. Fear hadn't been this strong in him since he'd been shot nearly a year ago now.

The power pouring off the two of them was great. It would be hot one second then cold as the deepest freeze the next. As they stood there, unmoving, he wondered what the people had been planning, and how the hell they thought they were going to get away with it. As soon as an elderly couple appeared in the room with them, the guards with Nildale surrounded them.

"That's it? That's all we had to do to figure this shit out?" Rider stood up as soon as the couple and guard were gone. "We've been here three days, three fucking days, and all we had to do was have Max and Murph come here and find them? This is really fucked up, you know that, right?"

"No, that's not all they had to do." Nildale slapped Rider across the face, a bold move for the former king, but it seemed to calm Rider down. "You're feeling the effects of the magic. Just take a few deep breaths and let them out slowly."

"I'm fine." Rider did sit down then, glaring at Nildale as he did so. "You didn't have to hit me, you know. You could have just told me to take it down a notch."

"You needed to be brought to focus. And let me tell you, it was sort of terrifying to do that to you." Rider nodded, but didn't look any happier about things. "The magic that they used, along with the magic of Linyah's that you still hold, has made you very tense. Not to mention a little on edge."

"I've been on edge my whole life." Misha had to agree with that one. But when Rider looked at him, he could see how upset he really was. And not just from the slap. "I'm sick of this shit, Misha. I don't mind helping out when necessary, but damn it, the criminals are getting stronger and smarter, and they're not playing by rules that we can follow. I want to be a husband, someday a father too. Not out running after people that have decided that their way is the better way. I'll help with family things. I have no problem with that, but I'm not going on these runs anymore."

"It's not always this way, Rider. But you're right. It is harder and harder to figure it out. Not just because of the magic used, but simply as you said, they're getting smarter and not playing by any rules." Nildale looked at Misha as he continued. "You have helped us out so much over the last few years. More than I can count, not only on this kind of events, but also on personal levels. If you'd allow it, I'd like to repay you."

"That's not necessary. We're glad to help you." Nildale said it was to him. "All right, but no more magic. I've been zapped by you before."

"Yes. Yes, you have. And while at the time I was nervous about it, now I think on it with humor. I hope you don't mind." Misha told him not so long as he didn't hurt him again. "No, not that. But I do have a nice gift for you all. And as soon as we're home again—yours, not mine—I'll present it to you. It's not much, just a decree stating that you are all as much my family as my blood children. I wish for there never to be any issues when you come and go."

"Thank you, but again, it's not necessary. We're family now, Nildale, and that's all that matters." Misha knew that no matter what he told him, Nildale would do as he pleased. The man, while a wonderful person, was used to getting his own way. "We'll have to deal with this. There are people out looking for these families still. And I doubt very much they'd care to hear they were plotting something against a king and queen of another realm that has been around longer than most rocks have. We have to have a story in place that people will believe and be able to settle in their minds on this."

"I have Linyah helping me with that. Nic, too. In a few hours people will simply forget that there was a fuss and that anyone was missing at all. The homes will be put up for sale; the contents of both the homes and campers will disappear and be donated to some charity as well. No one will remember the people or the things that went on here for the last few days." Misha asked what would happen to them. "Leila is taking care of them. They are her people, after all. And just so you know, they'll wish it was I that took them to task for this."

When Nildale shivered, as if whatever he knew was too much, Misha didn't ask. He knew that Leila was Murph's mom and Max's grandmother. But she was also a being that rarely tolerated people much, especially stupid ones. And she did not believe in second chances when it came to her family and being safe. He'd never want to cross her.

As they began gathering their things to go home, Rider pulled him aside. It was in his head to tell him not now, that he had enough to deal with, but he looked so serious. Misha suggested that they go to a diner and talk there.

"I'm done." Misha nodded. "I don't mean until the next one of these comes along, but I don't ever want to do this again. I thought I might. Even had it in my head that I could do smaller jobs on my own after we closed up shop. Then Graham came along and I fell in love. But this shit, this is too much, Misha. I don't even want to find a lost dog. I'm over people and the messes they can get into."

"You want a home life. I can understand that." Rider started to talk. "No, let me finish. I know that you want a home life. So do I. All of us do. And you're right. We either do this all the time, or not at all. And like you, I'm for not at all. It is too much. Even when it turns out good, which isn't often, it's the other ones, the really bad ones, which weigh us down so that even the good things seem as if there is trouble brewing. You're right, all or none, and I'm done as well."

"Good, I'm glad to hear that. I was afraid you'd say just give it time. I was serious when I said I wanted to be with my wife. We're going to travel some. See new places and try new things. I want to wake up in the morning in a comfortable bed beside her. Not in some hotel alone where I know that I'm either going to have to dig out bodies or take the risk of being shot up by one of the bad guys." Misha agreed with him. "I'm sorry."

"Don't be. I'm glad that you told me. I feel the same way." Rider nodded but didn't look convinced. "When I take this shirt off today, it, as well as the one with spit up on it, is going into the trash. I don't even want to have it in the house as a memory. Because, as you said, there aren't a lot of good ones associated with them."

"Thank you." Misha told him that he should be thanking him. "As soon as we take care of this dragon thing, Graham and I are going on a vacation. I told her to plan for a month. I want to see the places that she picks out for the two of us. I want to see them with her at my side."

"Good for you. If you don't mind waiting until we settle up with the plant coming in, then I will buy you your first vacation shirt." Rider said he could do that. "All right then, it's done. Right now."

As they boarded the plane, he told the others what was going to happen. He wasn't surprised to see relief in all their faces and to hear a few cheers of good news. It had been a good job, one that had brought them so much in terms of meeting some wonderful people, but enough was enough. They deserved this time.

~~~

Graham was pleased with the building. She thought her dad was as well. There were drying racks in the rafters as well as several sinks that he could work in. A long table had been put down the middle of the room that was made of the finest stainless steel she'd ever seen. And there were enough fans blowing slowly overhead that she knew that it would be great for drying whatever her dad brought in, as well as keeping him cooled.

"There's even a nice cot here should I like to sleep for a bit." She looked at the room that had been added to the plans she'd seen. The *cot* was a queen sized bed with a lovely handmade quilt on it. "And Rider made sure that I have a kitchen for my food as well as a nice lab to work in. The book, our book? It has its own special safe too. So that no ruffians get to it."

"You expect a lot of ruffians to come through here?" He just smiled at her. It was great to see her dad so happy. "I noticed that there is a garden going in as well. You should be able to grow whatever you want there."

"Yes. Sina has found some seeds too, ones that were in my garden all those years ago. And there are any number of them that I can buy online and at the corner store. I had no idea that things could be so easily taken care of and purchased." Graham wondered briefly if Sina had found him seeds or had them conjured for him, and decided that it didn't matter. Her dad was thrilled. "She's also given me a few from her own realm to use as I saw fit. Of course I've been talking to her gardener on what they do and how much work they can be. I don't want to harm

122

this world with things that could be bad."

As they finished up the tour of the building, they went into the large yard that sat far back from the house itself. As her dad talked about the garden again, Graham looked at the woods beyond them. That was when she saw the large wolf staring at her.

"Dad?" He turned to look when she did. "Is that James Luna? Or one of his pack? Rider said that they'd be on the land, but that one looks wrong."

The wolf came forward but not close enough to touch them. When he sat down on his hind end, Graham felt no less afraid for them. As soon as he laid down on his belly, his eyes never leaving theirs, she reached out for Rider and told him what was going on.

Can you command him? She asked him what she needed to do. *Just tell him to shift, and if he's one of James's men, then you should be able to do it. I'm on my way home now, but it might be another forty minutes or so.*

Graham knew that if she ordered this person to shift that they'd be in pain. But since he didn't seem to be in any kind of hurry to explain himself, she thought this might teach him a lesson. But before she could do more than try and figure out just how to do that, he stood up and moved toward her.

"Stop right there." He did so, of course, but he didn't lie down again. "Who are you and what are you doing here?" The laughter touched her mind first, then his words, still full of humor, didn't do much to quell her fear for her dad.

My name is Cyrus. You have never met me. I came as a wolf so that you'd not fear me. I can see now that you do just that. Would you mind asking Sina, or even any of the others, about me? I am the child of a man named Monroe. She didn't say anything, the names jogging a small memory but not enough to have her place the man. *You're Rider's mate. I know him as well.*

Nodding to the wolf, she spoke to Rider. *He said that he knows you. His name is Cyrus and his maker is Monroe.* Rider told her that he knew both men but to not take any chances. *I wasn't planning on it. My dad is here too.*

Ask him the name of the book he got from Laci for his birthday. She found him the first addition of Edgar Allen Poe's The Masque of the Red Death. *Also, what was inscribed in the book.* Graham thought about such a gift for someone, but knew that this family was very generous. *You are as well, my love.* She asked Cyrus the first of the two questions.

The Masque of the Red Death. *It's a beautiful copy. I have another of his,* The Raven, *which is a poem by the way. The other is in poor shape in comparison; the book itself, not the prose inside of it. And the inscription in the middle of the title page is made out to a man by the name of Wendell Cartwright.* The wolf laid down as he continued. *He wrote no words other than to the man, and then signed with his own name.*

"And you've come here for what reason? Not to scare us as you already said, but you have a reason, correct?" He stood up again, and this time when he stretched, she could see the man as he began to take the body of the wolf. When the man stood up, fully clothed she was glad to see, he bowed low before her. "You could have simply come to us as you are now."

"There are people about—not all of them working on this land but they are still about—that I thought it best that they don't know I'm here. I have been following such a man until I realized that he was the prospective renter for the land in town." She had heard that someone was coming to this area to open a warehouse. "He smells of wealth and has no outward feelings of deceptiveness. And he is inspecting the land I would imagine to see what he might not be told otherwise. I would do the same, as I'm sure you would have under the circumstances."

"Then he doesn't trust that Rider would be telling him the truth." Cyrus said that as the man knew very little about Rider, he could understand that. "I can too, but it doesn't make it any less aggravating that he's walking about without telling anyone. And that he's being sneaky about it."

"True. But he is only a man and is he making very little progress around the area. He is being thwarted, so to speak, by the good people protecting you and your family." She asked him what he meant. "He has run into some minor difficulties with the local pack, as well as a few shifters on the land that have had him running for his life. Not that they'd harm him, not without permission, but he is a stranger to them. And it's good that he understands that to trespass even under these circumstances might mean a little price is to be paid."

She supposed that was good too. With all the other crap going on, it was sort of nice knowing that not everything had to be taken care of right now. She'd have to think of something nice to give to the pack for helping. Graham wondered what Rider would say, and realized he'd probably already taken care of it. Looking up at the sky, she realized how bright the sun was and wondered for the man Cyrus.

"Would you like to come up to the house?" Cyrus told her that he couldn't enter but he would enjoy sitting with her on the porch. "Because of it being Rider's home? Or is it me?"

"Neither, as a matter of fact, but the house has been warded against all kinds that do not have your blood. Laci has been very generous to me, saving my life, but that does not extend to you and your mate." She asked him why not. "Because Laci is not a

Lanning by blood; none of the women are, I know, but permission has to be given by a blood Lanning and not a wife. It's the way the ward was set up."

"Oh. I see. I'm sorry." He bowed again. "Well, we can have a nice quiet time on the deck. My father, his name is Allister, by the way, is working on his gardens."

Cyrus nodded and walked to where her dad was pulling weeds. She knew the difference between weeds and herbs, but she wondered if the vampire did. When he knelt next to her dad and pulled a few of the right greenery, Graham knew he was a man who had helped in a garden before.

"You have a very nice one, my lord. And if you would like, I could bring you a few cuttings from our own gardens. I think you'll find a few that you do not have here." Her dad said that would be great. "Very good. I will ask Monroe to bring them when he comes later. After Rider is here."

She was sure it was going to be too bright for the vampire when he left the darkness of the woods, but he told her that he was very old, but not as old as his maker, and that he had developed the ability to be in sunlight just after being turned. As he walked beside her on the way to the house, he explained.

"There are a great many powers that come to a person after many years on this earth. As I'm sure you have found out as well." She told him she had worked hard at her craft. "And it shows. You are very strong for one so young."

"I'm not young." She realized what she'd said when he laughed. "Okay, I might be a little younger than you, but not by much."

"I am old, my lady. I was turned so long ago now that I cannot remember even the year, much less a date. Monroe is much older by that and more." She thought about the changes that he might

126

have seen, the horrors of life too. She knew, firsthand, that people had remained the same over the centuries. But their weapons, even verbal ones, had gotten worse. "I have made you sad."

"No. I'm sorry. I was thinking how sad things are, I guess. Thinking of all the things that I've seen and compared them to your own. We've witnessed a great deal, you and I. It's mindboggling to think how much it's changed, and hasn't too." He agreed. "But, we do what we can with what we had to work with. And for me, it wasn't so bad. For you, I would imagine, it was pretty terrible."

"I was with someone that abused his power over me. As it turned out, the Lanning family, Laci actually, rescued me. Had it not been for her, I don't think I would have survived." He paused in mid-step and she stopped moving as well. "Your man who was walking about the property, the one that I was speaking about, he is on your front porch. I don't think him to harm you, but you should call in some of the others."

Reaching for someone to help her out, Graham and Cyrus moved to the porch. She was pretty sure that the man was human, and Cyrus confirmed that. Graham told Hannah as well as Laci what was going on.

We're on our way to you. Don't let this little shit hurt you. Rider will never forgive us. But I just heard from Maribel. She's pretty close to you, I think. Hannah laughed. *She's hell on wheels lately, so you might have to rescue the buyer if he pisses her off.* Graham said she'd do her best, but wasn't going to make any promises.

As it turned out, Maribel was pulling in the drive when they reached the house. As soon as she got out, she looked at Graham with a gleam in her eyes that sort of scared her a bit. Whatever this man had going on, Graham was pretty sure that Maribel wasn't going to take any shit from him.

CHAPTER 10

Shadow hurt everywhere. Even his teeth were painful to chew with, and he'd lost two of them in the last week when he tried to eat a burger. Things were not going well for him. And he was pretty sure that very soon he was going to be dead.

He had no one to blame but himself in this. He could have, he supposed, blamed most of it on Sonya. But what would be the point of that? She was dead anyway, killed by her own hand more or less, and had paid the price of her greed as he was doing now. It didn't make him feel any better, but he didn't blame anyone for it. In fact, he had made peace with himself, and now he figured it was time to clean up some of his mess in this. Shadow touched the sigil on his hand and thought back to the day he'd woken with him there.

Sonya had been pacing the huge field. The wizard, or whatever he'd been, lay dead in the grass with him, his body mangled in a way that made Shadow sick to his belly. His body hadn't just been torn apart, but it looked as if it had also been burned, stabbed, and even chewed upon. He turned away from the mess when Sonya said his name.

"Finally. I had thought in addition to harming me, he'd killed my only hope in this. I need for you to wake sooner when you are given magic. This lying about like you did today will not work." He told her he was sorry before he could remember that he'd had nothing to do with what had happened to him. "The dragon is where I told you we'd put him. And so you know, he's not at all happy with this. Seems to me he'd be glad for the freedom he's getting from that dreadful cave he was in. But no one is ever grateful when you try your best to do things you know are right for them."

"I don't understand what you mean. Where is Draconal?" Shadow had looked around then, looking for the big dragon, when Sonya slapped him in the head. He felt something, a power roll over him, and he looked down at his hand when she jerked it to her. "You marked me?"

"No. I did nothing more than bring you here. The magic has marked you. See the wording around the dragon? That's the spell that holds him there. You must never allow anything to break that circle of magic or all hell will break loose. And I mean from me. I'll not have you messing with my plans after I've gone to so much trouble to have that dragon put there. I've had to do a lot of suffering in order for you to hold the dragon for me. And you will be respective of the things I've done for you." Shadow had glanced at the dead man. Sonya laughed, bitterly. "He allowed me to be injured. As his future queen, he should have taken better care. See?"

She lifted her sleeve up and he saw nothing there that would warrant such a death. It had taken her pointing to the small scrape on her arm, about the size of a pea, for him to see what she'd been upset about. Shadow remembered thinking that she'd show him more, let him see all that had been done to her, but she only stood there, staring at him.

"Have you healed over now?" She looked confused. "Surely you didn't kill that man for this wound. There had to be more of it, correct?"

"Nay, this is it. I cannot heal myself, as you are aware, but I have my own people that will care for such an injury when I return to my home." He looked at the mark again and wondered who in their right mind would think it was any more than a tiny hurt. "I don't like things to go wrong. He knew better when he hurt me. Not only did he wound me terribly, but in his haste to pull me out of the way of the rearing dragon, he mussed my clothing as well. I don't know what is wrong with people today. They have no respect for others' feelings or their things. I was there to make sure he did it correctly, not to be handled with such force. Don't you think?"

"He saved your life and you repaid him by killing him?" She just cocked a brow at him, as if to ask him if he'd really needed to ask her that. "I'm not sure this will work with us. What would happen if I made a mistake and harmed you trying to save your life? Would you murder me as well?"

"I murdered no one here, Shadow. I simply made an example of him. One that I think you can appreciate. Do not cross me. And as far as the two of us working together, there will be no breakup. We're together in this until every last Lanning and their brats are gone." He looked at the man, then at her again. "You are mine and as such, so is the dragon. When I call upon you, you will do as you're told or the death of that man will look like child's play."

He'd not crossed her in all the years he'd been her servant. It wasn't until later, after he'd seen what she did to a great many people that didn't comply with her demands, that he realized that he'd be better served to avoid her. But that hadn't worked out well either after a while.

Shadow hadn't wanted to be her lover. Not any woman's lover, as a matter of fact. He hadn't any idea what being a homosexual had been back in the beginning. Nor did he understand why he had more feelings about men than he did the opposite sex. Shadow had avoided both sexes for as long as he could until one day, a nightmarish week as it turned out, Sonya had told him that he would fuck her.

"I like my sex rough. And you will be my toy." He shook his head as he stood in her room he'd been brought to, and started to tell her that he wasn't interested in her like that. "I don't really give a good fuck if you are or not. But you will satisfy me or I'll feed you to the hogs."

"Hogs?" She grinned at him then. "You mean dogs, perhaps? You'll feed me to the hounds if I don't make you enjoy sex between us?"

"No, I meant what I said. Hogs. Did you know that they have no care whatsoever what they are fed so long as it fills their bellies? Why, just the other day I put a body in their pen, and within minutes they had not just devoured the thing, but all traces of his clothing and other items. It was so thrilling to me that I found two more for them just to watch them feed." He knew even then that he should have run. Or killed himself. But it had been too late, for everyone. "Now, you'll fuck me until I scream, and if you do a good job of it, I'll reward you with magic. If not, then you'll be hog feed for the next day. Do you understand me?"

"Yes."

He took off his clothing, folded it, and lay it neatly on the chair. He'd had so very little then, and had wanted to keep things in good repair. He should have taken more care of his body, for it was abused beyond what a normal man could have stood. But he'd lived to walk away, even if he did have a horrific limp afterwards.

Shadow moved to the pallet that he'd been resting on, dragging his memories from that hideous time. As he lay down, his body hurting more for just standing still, he lifted his hand up to see the mark there. Over the last several days he'd thought about cutting the circle and freeing the big beast. He might just yet, he thought, but for the fact that he had no idea what would happen to him when he did. Then there was the added fact that he wasn't sure if the thing would go after the Lannings. And above all else, Shadow had decided that he didn't want them to die. If the dragon killed him when freed, which was looking very promising, what would happen to Draconal? He hadn't been the nicest dragon he'd worked with, but he was smart and did a good job for the king and queen. What to do? What to do?

He missed Jim more and more daily. The man had been his friend and lover for so long, it was like he'd had a part of him cut away when he'd ended his life. He knew now that it was a good thing that he'd done. If not, then he would have had to watch him suffer. Jim would have done the same thing for him, he knew that. Shadow also knew that his own fate was going to be no less painful for him, but to have had Jim there with him, he knew that they would've worked something out. Even if it meant freeing the dragon.

"I don't know how to even do that." He looked at the circle and knew that if he could only read the words there, it would be the key he was looking for. Not to save his own ass, but to let the dragon go. He should never have been trapped like he was in the first place; Shadow knew that now. "Now look at me. I'm broken and broke. I've lost everything I had, including friendship, and I have no one to talk to about it."

What would he say to someone should they be right there with him, he asked himself? Oh, how do I let a dragon go that has been trapped in my body for longer than you've been living? Or a better question might be, do you know how to get in touch with the king and queen of another realm so that I might tell them how sorry I am that I fucked up? Yes, Shadow thought, that would go over well. The longer he lay there, the more depressed he became. He'd had such a wonderful life until Sonya.

~~~

Maribel felt out of sorts, like she should run or stay all in the same heartbeat. The human, Walker Knight, seemed like a very nice man, but she just didn't know what to say to him. When she heard her name being said, she looked at Graham, who had a glass of lemonade in her hand.

"Thank you, child." Her fingers burned to touch something. Maribel turned to Walker to see if he could please explain to her what the hell he was doing there. But her thoughts evaporated when she watched him drink his lemonade.

The way that the condensation slid down the glass, the ice moving toward his mouth, made her warm all over. When he swallowed, the way his Adam's apple moved up and down like a bobber on water had her shifting on her seat. When he had drained the glass and set it on the small table, Maribel found herself wanting to pick it up again and lick the rim where his mouth had been. Christ love a dog, I am nuts, she told herself.

"I sure do love homemade lemonade." Maribel nodded, not sure she had even tasted hers to know if it was water or some other concoction. "Miss Maribel, you were asking me about the plant I'm having brought here. Well, I can tell you that I think I'm gonna do it. The ground would have to be ripped up, of course.

A building the size that I want to expand the existing— Are you all right, my dear?"

"I don't know. I just don't know." She looked at Graham, feeling well over her head right now. "I don't think I'm feverish, do you? I'm running hot and cold like I've got the flu."

"No, I'm pretty sure you don't have the flu." There was a hint of something there, something that made Maribel angry, but before she could lash out at the younger woman, she spoke again. "Perhaps you'd feel better if you sat on the swing with Walker. There is plenty of room."

Before she could object to such a thing, Walker moved to the side and patted the cushion. She didn't want to be rude or anything, so she found herself seated next to the big man. And in actuality, she did start to feel a good deal better after that.

"Walker, perhaps you can tell us a little more about yourself. Like, have you a family that will be moving out here with you?" He shook his head, and Maribel felt the relief of his actions all the way to her toes. "I'm betting that you'll be staying back where you are then? I mean, there is really no reason for you to move here to this little town."

"I already purchased a house and hired a few servants to help me out. Such a lovely home too, more than I would have gotten for the same price at home. I knew almost as soon as I stepped off the plane three days ago that I'd love living here full time. Of course, I did have a look around the place, got to know some of the people hereabouts too. I was pleased as punch when I saw how much development is going on. Even had a nice walk around those new shops that opened. Shoot-fire, I love those old pieces, and hope to get a few of them for my home." Maribel found that she loved the way the man spoke, his accent just enough to have her wanting to hear him say more. But when

135

he turned to her, sadness in his voice, she wanted to pull him to her and hug him. "My family is all gone now. My wife, rest her soul, died some years back, a long time ago now, and I've been by myself all this time. I have a staff that helps me out, but they're not family. Not like you have here. I bet you guys raise up a ruckus when you're all together."

"Oh my yes, we do. I have six boys, and six of the best daughters-in-law you can imagine. And grandchildren coming now too." She felt her face heat up at the way she'd gushed about her family. "I'm sorry about your own, Walker. I don't know how I would have survived without mine here all the time."

"Don't you worry your pretty little head about it. Not one bit. You should be proud of them. Working the world to have some extra businesses come here to help out the town. Every time I talked to Rider, all I could think about was his momma had raised him right. He's a good man." Maribel nodded, feeling her pride in her sons double in that moment. "I'm looking forward to working with each and every one of them. I'm to understand that this is a family venture, correct?"

"Oh yes. Rider was the one doing the research for them, but we all had a hand in getting things planned out." She looked over at Graham before continuing. "Do we take him out to the site or wait on my boys?"

"I have to wait on someone coming by. You should take him out." Maribel shook her head but Graham plowed on. "You know as much about it as anyone, Maribel. And can answer questions that he might have. Rider and the rest of them, they're going to be a bit later than they thought. So you take him out and if they return before you're done, I'll send them out there."

"Wonderful." Before she could find another reason why she didn't mean to take him out on her own, she found herself in the big limo that Walker had arrived in and sitting on the long bench seat with him. "This is going to be great. I've been wanting to go on out there and have a look-see, but I encountered a few of the wildlife out and about and didn't venture far. I suppose they're friends of yours too? Shifters and the like."

Maribel was aware that he knew what they were. Rider hadn't had to tell him, but the man knew. And when he'd been asked if that bothered him, apparently Walker had thought it funny and told Rider that he would rather work with shifters over humans any day, as they were not just easier to get along with, but also didn't generally pull any punches when they talked to you.

"Yes. The local pack has been roaming the land since before the building that is there was built. I'm not sure what the shape of the building is, but I know that at one time it was considered to be well made and up to date on all electrical, as well as modernization." She told him the specs of the building. "Rider said that you have all the other information. Do you have any questions for me before we get there?"

"Yes. I'd very much like to have permission to kiss you." Maribel looked at Walker, her heart pounding so hard in her chest that she put her hand over it to make sure it wasn't going to fall out. "You're about the most beautiful creature I've ever seen. And I have the most powerful need to taste your lips and mouth that it's about all I can think around. What do you think, Miss Maribel? Would you let me have a taste of what you have there?"

"You don't know me." He nodded and cupped his hand to the back of her head. "You might be very disappointed in me. I'm not much of a woman."

"I don't even think that's possible. And you're more woman than my poor heart can take, I'm thinking." His mouth touched hers, gently and warmly. Her body screamed at her, her cat

137

clawed at her skin for her to take more. "I can feel her there, your cat. All I can think of now is seeing you as her."

"I'm not sure that that's a good idea either." He pulled her to him again, her body to his, pressed about as intimately as a couple could get. And when he shifted her, pulled her over his lap so that she was facing him, Maribel ran her hands over his hard muscles and down his back. "Touch me, Walker. I need you."

His hands were everywhere, undressing her, his mouth touching her in places she'd not had anyone see in decades. Maribel's breath caught when his mouth tugged at her nipple. Holding him to her, feeling her body warm, heat for him, all she could think about was having him fill her, to take her. And when she was rolled to the seat, his body over hers, Maribel knew he was going to take her right there and then. It was then that it hit her.

"You can't be." He said nothing as he pulled his shirt up and over his head. "No, wait, you have to understand something. There's been a mistake. I've been mated before. I have the boys there to prove it. This is wrong, so wrong."

"There's been no mistake, love. I know what you are to me. You're my mate." She nodded, sure he was going to tell her that she was wrong. "I have never felt this way before. Heard about it. How there isn't any way to stop from needing the other half of you. I never understood it until I saw you standing there next to your car with fire blazing from your eyes. My goodness woman, you looked good enough to eat. I just might have to before this is all done."

"But I have already had my mate. He was a bastard, yes, but he was the only one for me." Walker slid his hand up under her skirt and touched his finger to her wetness. "Don't do this. You have no idea what this is going to mean to us. I'm not going to do this with you right now. You have to know this is wrong. So very wrong."

"It's not wrong, darling. We're meant to be together. And I don't care that you had another man in your life. What I care about is that he's gone. He is, isn't he?" She nodded as he touched her clit through her panties and moaned. Her head was having a hard time keeping up with his words. "I'm going to bring you. Let you come all over my fingers, then I'm going to lick them clean of you. Then if you'd allow it, I'm going to pull you over my lap and have you ride me cowboy style. Having that pussy of yours wrapped all around me is about all I can think of right now."

She covered her mouth with her hand when he slid his fingers under her panties and into her. The scream that seemed to want to escape took her breath away, as did her release. And as he brought her a second, then a third time, she was so needy that she nearly pounced on him when he lifted her up from the seat.

Her body was bared for him. And for some reason she couldn't explain, she didn't feel embarrassed by it. The way that he looked at her, touched her now, made her think she was lovely, beautiful even. Maribel hadn't felt that way...well, she wasn't sure that she'd ever felt that way in all her life. And when he freed his cock for her, Maribel wanted to touch him, needed to. Moving her fingers along the length of him, her hand wrapped around his girth, she was careful not to harm him as she explored him.

"What I wouldn't give to have you beneath me right now, the two of us in a big bed. My cock buried deep within you, having you tighten around me over and over as you came." Walker rolled his hips up, his cock filling her hand as he thickened more. "I need you, baby. I want to feel you around me."

It took some doing to get her over him. On her knees she slid down over his cock as slowly as she could, needing to feel every inch of him. The way he felt made her moan, the stretching of her pussy made her wetter. And when she was seated over him, his cock filling her like Andy never had, she held onto Walker's shoulders as he suckled at her breasts.

"Ride me, darling. I want to feel you have your pleasure before I take my own. And know that I'm gonna watch you, see how your face looks when you're coming for me." She nodded, no longer sure she could stop herself even if she tried. "That's it, baby. Ride me hard."

Her movements were unsure, she knew this. Having never done this before, not just riding him but having sex in a moving vehicle, she tried to think of only him and his pleasure. But when he held her hips, showing her what he needed, what they both needed, Maribel's body began to hum, her need spiraled out of control once again. And when he bit down on her breast, just hard enough to remind her he was there, she came so hard that she saw stars, flowers, and rainbows all at once.

"Again. Come for me again." She had no choice in the matter. Maribel had had her doubts about being his mate, but when he commanded her to release, she did just as he wanted. Her body bowed back as he licked his way down her body to her ribs. "Christ, I need you."

She found herself on her back, Walker between her legs as he filled her. Every stroke of his cock, every time he touched something deep within her, she fell deeper in love with him. Her body now belonged to him as much as her heart did. And when he cried out that he was coming, she pulled him to her and bit hard on his throat, tasting the heated passion of their lovemaking the moment his blood filled her mouth.

Offering him her own throat, he seemed to understand quickly what she wanted. As soon as his tongue touched her pulse in her neck, she knew that she was going to come hard, her body would forever belong to him. When his teeth sank into her, his cock emptied at the same time and Maribel came hard enough to feel the world blank out.

When she woke, Maribel found herself in the back of the limo alone. Her heart ached for that. She knew that after he'd given her so much he'd find her lacking, and that he was even now regretting what they'd done. Gathering up her courage after pulling clothing on with her magic, she sat there for several minutes before she opened the door to get out. No matter what happened now, she told herself, she would at least have this one memory, a wonderful memory to keep her warm at nights.

"Hello, beautiful." Maribel felt her face heat up when Walker pulled her to him and kissed her. "I was worried that you'd not be able to join me here. I told Mike here that you were resting up."

"Yes. I was. I've been working so hard on different projects that I just fell asleep." She was babbling and Maribel was pretty sure that the other man knew it. When Walker kissed her again, enjoying the moment, she suddenly didn't care what anyone thought about her. "I should take you through the building and lands. I'm supposing you'll be leaving soon."

Walker asked Mike, the driver, if he'd give them a moment. "Did I hurt you, darlin'? Harm you in any way back there?" She shook her head, her heart too raw to speak. "Good. I'm glad to be knowing that. Surely I am. Because as of the moment I met you, I knew that I was never leaving here again. Not without you with me, at any rate. And I'd very much like for you to be with me all the time. I know this might sound crazy to you, but I'm head over heels in love with you."

"I don't think.... To be honest with you, Walker, I don't think I could have lived without you here with me. And I'm in love with you as well. I've never felt this way before for a man. Not in all my life. I'm so nervous one moment and all excited the next that I feel like a school girl on her first outing. I had worried that you'd left me or found me lacking in some way." She felt the tears that she'd not shed in the limo fall. "This is all so new to me, you have no idea. I was terrified that I'd disappointed you somehow."

"Disappointed? Oh darling, you near about killed me. I cannot wait to take you to those heights and beyond in a real bed. I can almost see it now, a big one so we have plenty of room to play. And we're going to play a lot, you and I. I've been waiting for you my whole life, and I'm not going to let any time go by without being with you. The things I have planned for that wonderful body of yours." She nodded, feeling like a young woman again. "Now, let's me and you get this all cleared up so that we can go on back to my hotel room and have us a good old time. We might be there a few days. I know you gotta tell your family about us. I understand that. So you go on and do that now. If they wanna meet me before I take you, then that's all right too. But no matter what, you're all mine."

Maribel liked the sound of that, very much so. And when she reached out to tell Graham, knowing that she'd let the others know, it occurred to her that she might have known what was going on before they left. As soon as she laughed when she told her what was going on, Maribel knew it.

You, of all the people I know in this world, deserve this the most. Yes, I'll tell the others. And you have a wonderful time. She laughed again. *We won't expect the two of you tonight, but tomorrow night we'll be having that big dinner before we talk to the dragon. Bring Walker too. He might as well get to know the real us.* Maribel said that she would. *Good. And you might want to explain to him that he's going to be around a lot longer than he thinks. That might go a long way to making him okay with leaving the hotel room for a little while.*

I will. And tell the boys to behave themselves or I'll tan their hides. Graham told her to leave them to her. *You keep them in line, child. Tell them.... Well, you tell them that I've never been so happy. And that I want them to be happy for me. I need this. I think I've needed this man in my life for a very long time.*

And she was happy too. Maribel Lanning was as happy as she'd ever been in her life.

Chapter 11

"And you're saying that this will work?" Rider didn't care for the look Allister gave him. It was a cross between why are you asking and who knows. "I don't want anyone hurt. Especially Graham. So if you're having doubts now, this would be a good time to voice them."

"I don't have any doubts that this will work. And if there is pain, she'll take it better than most. And you too. But I'm thinking, hoping really, that no one gets any kind of pain." Not an answer. Sort of a roundabout way of telling him that he wasn't sure of shit. Before he could ask Allister if they could put this off until he had better odds, he spoke again. "The dragon is gonna have to know that we're there for him. Otherwise he's going to come out and kill whatever is in his way. The poor thing has been trapped there for a very long time. I have wondered if he has any idea what is going on around him. Poor thing. I hope he'll be all right with this."

"That's why the king and queen are here. I'm to understand that they had a very good relationship with him before this all happened. Nildale said he could calm him well, but Sina would do a better job." Allister nodded but looked sad. "This is going to be all right, Allister. The dragon won't harm anyone and he'll be free. You're doing a good job here for him. Right?"

"Yes. He will. And that person of Shadow's that was living with has left him alone in this world too. You could almost feel sorry for Shadow. Almost. But that just doesn't make it right that he has to be killed. I know that he's not been the most stellar of people all this time, but you know how she was. Sonya would have done this to him, with or without his permission, and the man would have had to comply or die." Okay, Rider thought, there was that. "I'm thinking that without his ability to use the magic that he gained from Sonya, he's hurting. And will be more every day. His body will be aging, falling into disrepair. Then there is the fact that he has no money, no one to get help from. Nic said that he's living in one of the buildings in the downtown area, living there so as not to draw any unwanted attention to himself. Not hurting anyone, but just staying to himself. I'm thinking he's close to giving it all in now to try and hurry his ending. It's what I would do, if I was hurting like I bet he is."

"And that would be bad how?" Rider knew, because he'd asked the same thing a few hours ago, when talking with Allister about what was going on. But his family, Misha included, was not as up to speed as he was. "If he's dead then this ends, right?"

"No, it will not end. The dragon will die with him. And nothing will be resolved." He could see the look on Misha's face. It said, so what, he'd be dead, but Rider knew that it was not right. "The dragon, Draconal, is the first of his kind. Created so long ago no one knows the date. And now he's trapped within a being against his will and expected to kill people that were not known to him. It would be unfair, of all of us, to kill him for no reason. To end his life because of the greed and stupidity of someone else."

"I can see that. I just.... If you want to know the truth of it, I'm nervous about all of this. It just seems too easy to simply say some words and he's free. And has anyone thought of what we're to do with a large dragon? I have, and I can't think of a single way to make this work." Allister laughed and everyone turned to him. Misha stood up, ready no doubt to tear into the man if the look on his face was any indication. "You think this is funny? That we might care about the other people of the world here?"

"Nay, I didn't mean that. But you're assuming things that just aren't there to worry about." Misha asked him what he meant. "First, the dragon is large. Yes, larger than any creature you might have encountered in this realm. And magical. He has more magic than all the witches, warlocks, and wizards put together on both this realm and the one he came from. Not just in his abilities, but his body as well. Every part of a dragon, even his scales, is used for more magic should you be able to gather them."

"How is that helpful?" Rider watched Allister as he struggled to answer him. Instead of giving him time to do so, Rider asked him what he'd been thinking of for days now. "If he's so powerful, why doesn't he just free himself?"

"Ah, there is the rub, isn't it? Like all beings, there are certain ways to trap him. Like you with the people who wish to harm you. They need only to find your weakest spot and use it against you. And for you that would be Graham. They would take her to lure you into some area. The way that they'd hold you there, make you do things that are against anything you'd ever do, is to continue to hold the threat of harm over those that you love." Rider asked him if the dragon had a family. "He does. A great many offspring that he loves and holds dear to his heart, just as much as you do yours. So they trapped him, and in order to keep them safe he did as he was told. And his family is safe, so far as I know."

"How do you know this?" Rider watched as Allister struggled again with an answer. "You've talked to the other dragons, his family, haven't you? You found out exactly what they did to him to bring him under their control."

"As I have said, he's the father to all dragons. His life for theirs was a small price to pay for them. Same as it would be for you, I would imagine." Rider nodded. "His child was there with them when he was captured within Shadow's body. She said that it was so painful for her father that she hurts still to this day thinking about what he suffered for them all."

"So he lives where he is, not harming his host, because he doesn't want his family hurt. What has changed? Why is he so ready to come out now?" Allister said that he didn't know other than he might be aware of Sonya's death. "And I'm sure that Shadow isn't helping him much either. Didn't you say that the dragon feeds off the magic of Shadow? With him having less and less of it, does that mean he'd feeding from the man himself?"

"Yes, that's as good a reason as any. Until he's free, we can only speculate as to what he's doing and why. But Draconal is slowly killing the man who holds him, and in turn, killing himself as well. Thus the reason for the need to hasten this talk with him. When the host is dead, there is a good possibility that Draconal might die as well. And that would be a great tragedy." Rider nodded. He had figured out already that the dragon was killing the man, but the consequences of this hadn't occurred to him. "So, we're ready? We can do this now?"

"Yes. We're ready if you are." Rider nodded and then looked at Graham, who nodded as well. They all headed out the door of

the house, only to be brought up short by the man standing there.
~~~

Shadow didn't move. Not that he could, he supposed, but he was pretty sure if he had, he'd have been killed. Not just by the cats in front of him, but the wolves behind him as well. He'd been both surprised and relieved to find how easy it was to get them to help him. Once he spoke with the alpha of the pack, they'd been pretty nice about escorting him here. The few nips to his body were a small price to pay to his way of thinking. He had invaded their territory.

Clearing his throat, something that he'd not been able to do for a very long time, he tried to think what he had to say. He was ever so thankful to the young queen for allowing him to speak again when he'd requested an audience with her. But he had to make this right. However he could.

"I've come to hand over Draconal. He's sick, I think. We both are, and I'd like someone to see to him. I'm here to give him over, if you think you can take him from me." The taller man nodded, but didn't say anything. "I'm human. Or I used to be. A very long time ago. But I think you're the one in charge. The wolf behind me, he said so long as I wasn't stupid that he'd allow me to get this far. I hate to say it, but I think I've been stupid for pretty much most of my life. I need to make amends for that now."

"Amends? I don't know how you think that's going to work. You've been around long enough to know that what you've done is beyond stupid." Shadow told him that he knew that as well. "I'm Misha Lanning. You must be Shadow. Why are you here? If you think to kill us, you're sadly mistaken on that part."

Shadow was glad for the man's straightforwardness. He also liked the fact that, as a group, the family seemed to be beside him. Shadow wondered if Jim were here, whether he'd tell him he was doing the right thing or tell him to run. Probably both.

"No. I have no reason to wish you harm. I have caused enough in my life to last several lifetimes. I come to you to give you what rightfully wasn't ever mine in the first place. To give you your lives back as best I can." He glanced at the men and women there, all of the men related, he knew, and could feel their hatred, their confusion as well. The women, their counterparts and other halves, were angry as well, not that he blamed them. "I'm not laying all the blame at her feet, but Sonya told me to end your lives. That to do so would make me the greatest man alive. I came to realize, even before her death, that her ideas were less than well thought out, and that she had grand plans with no means of carrying them through. I believe I was one such dream. Her need to have your lives ended and the way she schemed to have it carried out has hurt more people than you can ever imagine. The lives lost to her cause, the way she manipulated people to do her bidding, would astound you. And while I was not a willing partner in her plans, I was a partner all the same. And for that, I can only beg you to end my life quickly. Please."

"You said that you've brought us the dragon, that you wish him to be free. Why this sudden change of heart? Last we heard, you had a plan to come here and end all our lives. Why now? Why this way?" This man he had seen in Sonya's visions; the last of the men to become mated with his other half. "I'm Rider. This is my mate, Graham."

"I know you. Of you anyway. You're the man I was to take, and then kill your mate after she freed the dragon from me. I was never clear on how that was to work, but Sonya assured me that when the time came, I'd know." Shadow asked to have a seat and limped his way to the rocker on the porch. "It's why I'm here, to tell you what I know and to, as I have said, give you the dragon. I would have at one time said I was here to fulfill a dream. But not so much lately. I've come to empty my head of sorts, and to have my heart cleansed as well. Draconal does not deserve what has been done to him. And neither do you all."

"And you? What do you think of what happened to you? And I'm going to tell you right now, it's not right of you to think that, just because you're here now with a sad story, we can forgive you for this. You tried to kill us. How many lives have you ruined in this quest of yours?" Shadow had thought they'd ask him this, wonder at his thoughts in coming here. He had no more answer to that than he did why Sonya had done this to him. "I can read your mind, you know."

"Yes, I know. I know a great many things about you that Sonya prophesied. I don't know that much of it has come to pass, but if you'd not mind, I'll share what she told me." Rider nodded. "You're to be a great man in your own right. A man of men, it will be said. You and your mate will sire many children, all of them as smart as their parents. And some day, in the not too distant future, you raise up this family to the heights that it should have been all those centuries ago, when the first of your kind turned Sonya down to become her familiar."

"His name was Rider too." Shadow nodded, glad that he'd not have to say too much. His strength was waning. "Sonya killed his family to make him comply with what she wanted. Little did she know that he was stronger than any magic that she had."

"She did at that. By doing what she did to him, she set in motion a chain of events that would never end the way that she wanted it to. Rider was a good man...this other Rider, I mean. He cared for his aging family and even the people in his town. But Sonya wanted to show off, bring herself a leopard to the mix so that Sina, the then queen, would be so impressed that she had one that she'd just lay down her crown and allow Sonya to rule. But Rider had no desire to work with her. You're a great deal like him in that respect. Kind, intelligent, as well as good with people. And by all accounts strong too. There have been exceptions to the strength and character of the Lanning men, but for the most part, each generation became more until they begat you men." He wondered if they knew he meant their father, but could see on their faces that they did. "Your father was no less taken in by Sonya than I was. But you must know that without him in your lives, even after he sired you, you would not be the men you are now."

"Hard to think of the good he brought about to our family when he was nothing but an abusive prick." Shadow looked at the older woman standing beside Misha when he spoke. When she laid her head on the chest of the man behind her, he could see love there. She had found her other half. "My father only took and never gave. And even when he took everything that we had, he wanted more. Felt that he deserved the best no matter who had to suffer because of what he wanted."

Shadow nodded and felt they needed to know it all, every detail of the plan that Sonya had had for them. Shifting on the seat, he looked at them all and studied the face of the man he had come to admire. In the last few moments, Shadow had decided that Rider was indeed going to be the best of the best of these men.

"I want you to know something. I think it's important for you to know the lengths that Sonya went to so that she could have what she wanted. When your parents first met, all those years ago, Sonya approached him, begged him not to sire any children. But the man was so besotted with his wife and the prospect of being a father that he turned her down flat. And you know how well that went over. So she put a curse on him, one that, on a few occasions, he was able to break free from. But it was too much for him and he succumbed to her ways. Andrew was to beat his wife to death before any children were born to her." He could see the shocked looks on their faces. Instead of looking at them, he looked at the mother that had borne them. "You were never to have lived past the wedding night. Sonya had worked hard on having that happen, and when it didn't, she went into such a rage that Andy felt it for months after. The magic that surrounded him should have had him murder you with a knife, then he was to take his own life, ending the Lanning line even before it began. It was going to be her greatest victory. To have you all dead before you were even a thought."

"He tried to strangle me. That night after we'd...he had gotten so angry with me. I don't even remember what it was about or even if it was that much. But it was minor in comparison to his anger at me. I tried to get away from him, tried to escape, but it wasn't until he saw the blood on my face that he told me, begged me, to run. And I did, never looking back as I went home to my parents." She sat down now, right across from him. "As a mate, he wasn't supposed to be able to harm me. After I went back to him, I thought for years that we weren't supposed to be together. Not be man and wife. But then the boys started to come along and I was happy with them. I never understood why he, my own mate, could cause me so much harm, and for nothing more than loving him. I did too...loved him with all that I was. But after a while, even that died out."

"He knew this. He knew even then that he wasn't doing the best he could for you and the children. It tore at him too. And every time Sonya would go to him, strengthen her hold on him, he would fight her with all that he was. I believe that it was the main reason that he quit you all. So that he could save you in his own way." The man, her mate, put his hands on her shoulders. Her sons gathered around her like they were protecting her. From him? He had no idea, but it made him feel better just being able to clear some things up for them. But he wouldn't hurt her. Not any of them now. "I spoke to him once, not long before he disappeared from your lives. He told me that he hated himself, and that someday soon he was going to be murdered by his son. Andy never liked what he'd done to you. Never. He was just as hurt by Sonya as the rest of you were. And I think, in his own way, that coming to you, causing an uproar, was to get you angry enough to end his life. He told me that he was as proud as any father could be of his sons, but he was never able to tell any of you. Andy had been a good man; you need to know that. It wasn't easy for him to be the man that she made him."

The pain took his breath away. As he doubled over with it, he could hear them shouting at him to tell them what they could do. There was nothing, he was as good as dead now. Sitting up and being handed a glass of water he could not drink, he looked at Maribel.

"I must tell you everything." She nodded, tears in her eyes. "He never stepped out on you. There were no other women. He hurt for the pain he caused you and your children, hurt more because he did not understand why he'd do such a thing. Why she'd be making him do this to his family. He loved you all so very much. So much so that he wanted his life ended because he had no understanding."

"I killed him." The young woman stepped forward. "He was demanding that she let him into the house so that he could talk to her. He attacked and I had no choice but to save her. Maribel is the nicest person I know and she didn't deserve to be treated that way by him. He was beyond cruel to her."

"He was, but you have to understand that it wasn't his doing. And when you killed him, you saved them both." The pain became too much, blood pouring from his nose and eyes as he fell forward again. He was nearly finished, he told them, ready to end this. "The dragon, he will need someone to go to. Draconal has suffered long enough. I think you all have."

"You mean our bodies?" The panicky sound of the man's voice brought a much needed smile to his face. "I thought we were freeing him. You mean one of us have to have him in our bodies?"

"You are to free him. And no, you won't take him the way I have him now. What I meant was, he needs someone to take him home." Shadow wiped at the blood and saw the mark on his hand. "I cannot read this. Sonya said that you've only to open the circle and he'll be free. Hurry. If I die, he does as well."

Shadow felt his body being moved. The ground beneath him was cool to his fevered body. He wondered why they'd not taken him into their home, and remembered the size of Draconal. This was by far the best place for him to be when he was free. A woman stood in front of him; he knew her, the queen. If he could have, he would have bowed before her, begged her to end his life.

"I am truly sorry, my lady. If I could do it over, I probably would have done things much the same way, but I was tricked. As a great many people were." She said nothing but nodded. "Sonya told me such tales of you and the family. And I thought to protect the dragons. But I was caught up in her plans so deeply that I think I convinced myself I was doing the right thing. I wish now only that you keep the dragons safe."

"The dragons are safe now. And once Draconal is home, they'll be better for it. You did this for them and him. For that

155

you have my gratitude, Shadow, trainer of dragons." He felt her touch, the magic that had been his long ago entering his body. "You will not live, I fear. There is little I can do to save you now. Had you come sooner, I would have—"

"I don't deserve to be saved, my lady. As well you know." He felt the pain roll over him, not in waves but like he was being run over with it. Rolling to his side, the pain of it was so much that he puked and blacked out for a second. Blood spilled from his lips when he rolled to his back again. "Take care of him for me, my lady. Rider, he will make a good keeper if you should find yourself in need of one. His family was doing it long before I was ever the one that had been chosen."

"I believe you might be right about that. But it will be his decision, not mine to make. I will not have people run over as Sonya would have done to get what she wanted." As the world darkened, his body felt heavy. Shadow tried to tell them to hurry, time was running out. But then he saw him, a sort of shadow of Draconal. "I'm so sorry. I should never have agreed to this madness. Had I known even half of what I did after that night, I would never have done this to you."

You have harmed so many in your pursuit to have your own way. And you can say that Sonya was the leader, but you know as well as I that you could have simply walked away. Shadow told him again how sorry he was. *This family, they have been a good one. Better than most humans I have seen. And yet you were ready to destroy them because of a woman that had no more right to end their lives than you did in taking mine away from me.*

You're right. I have no excuse for what I did. I was a pawn in her plans, yes, but as you said, I could have walked away. Or ended my own life. These men are more than good ones. They're the kind that will go far in life, make things better for all. Shifters with great wealth and heart. *There isn't enough of that in the world, any world, anymore. You know this as well.* The dragon nodded at him. *You will care for them? They deserve it more than anyone that I have ever encountered. I have nothing to give them, no riches to leave them, but I would ask that you make sure that they want for nothing. They deserve it all.*

The queen has given them much more than you could have. Their blood is now together; their families are as one. As it should be. Shadow said he knew that, but that didn't mean that others wouldn't seek to harm them. *No harm shall come to them. Not so long as I have breath in my body and strength in my wings. You can rest assured that I will care for them as I have my own family. Forever and a day.*

Closing his eyes, Shadow could imagine them when the dragon came to help them. The look on their faces when he bowed before them. Opening his eyes, he saw her again, the queen he had served before the daughter. But it was impossible to tell her how sorry he was any longer. His body was too weak to even form a word.

"Go in peace, Shadow. I have taken care that you have the death befitting a dragon trainer. Your family will know that you have fulfilled your destiny and that you are at peace once again. You have given much to the Lanning family in your final act of kindness. To mine as well." He felt the tears roll down his cheeks. He knew that there was blood in them; everything he was seeing was tinged with it. "When you have been freed of the magic and dragon, your body will disappear. I have notified all that you are to be respected with your name among the others there, and they will abide by this for me. You have hurt a great many people and it will be difficult for them to understand. But I have explained to them what a brave and wonderful thing you have done for us. You will have your peace."

They'd never believe her. He knew how much pain he'd

caused them as well. When someone took his hand in theirs, he looked at Rider. He was so much like his namesake that it took his breath away.

"Dragon Draconal, come forth." Before the words were finished, the beginning of the chant to free him, Shadow could feel him moving. The dragon gathering his strength to leave his confinement. "Come now. Join us so that we might care for you."

There was no pain. He was sure had he not already started to close his own body down that there might have been. But as it was, all he felt was the flight of something wonderful getting ready to leave him. And when he knew that the dragon was ready, Shadow felt good. He'd done this, freed the great dragon before he too was dead.

Draconal left him then, his body, magically stored within him, simply lifted from him and was gone. Shadow looked at the dragon he'd not seen in real life for more years than he could remember. He was just as magnificent as he'd always been.

Draconal stood on his legs and spread his wings, the brilliant purple of his scales sparkling against anything that was near it. There was weakness about him, Shadow could see it. He'd failed him too, he realized, when he'd lost his magic that day. As the dragon leaned down to him, his hot breath near his face, Shadow closed his eyes.

Shadow was nearly dead now and he was sure that the dragon knew it. But he didn't harm him, as he was well within his rights to do. Shadow would have welcomed it from him, as a matter of fact. Opening his eyes, he was in awe of the creature. He closed his eyes again when it was too much to see such beauty, a beauty that he had nearly destroyed. As his body began to close down, his legs no longer working, his fingers touching nothing as they laid over his chest, Shadow thought of the Lannings and how much they had yet to offer the world. And because of his greed and stupidity, he was never going to see it. It was only fitting that he should not be a part of their glory.

~~~

Rider knew the moment that the man had passed away. His body, spent and riddled with weakness, had simply given up. When the dragon lay down beside him, his size much bigger than Rider had realized, the two of them stayed near the man who had died to give birth to a new generation of their family. The dragon blew his hot breath over the body of his keeper, and they both watched as instead of burning like he would have thought, his body simply disappeared.

You will be my caregiver, will you not, young Rider Lanning? Rider told Draconal that he wasn't fit to be a caregiver for anyone right now. *But you will do it all the same. Your ancestors, they did much for my kind. Not at the front lines, but behind us, keeping us well fed when we returned from battles. Our wounds taken care of so that we'd heal. The Lanning men, for all their being so young to our realm, they did much.*

"No. Not the Lannings. We've been here our whole life." Draconal only smiled at him. For all his teeth showing, he was quite beautiful. "My family has only just learned of the other realm. My brother, he encountered the genjar when we were working. You might have it a little messed up, but we've been here all along."

Nay. You and your brothers only just learned of the other place. You do realize that your family did not start with your mother and father? Young Rider, the first one, he was there with me. His wife, children, and their children took care of us. After a time, the name Lanning had disappeared, but he was there, and his family became mine over time. Rider looked down at the scorched ground of Shadow and it

159

occurred to him what the dragon was saying. *I can see that you've worked it out. Shadow is the grandson of the first Rider. He is the last of the Lanning seed that cared for us before you begin. You will be the next great family, the continuation of Lanning men caring for us dragons.*

"He was our relative?" Draconal told him he was. "He came here to kill us and he was related to us? How is that even possible? He wasn't even a leopard. He was...he said that he was human."

I do not believe that he made the connection in his life to what he had in way of blood to you. Young Shadow, he was as much abused as your father was. More so, I think, because he lost so greatly. And as you know, over the many years between the first Rider and this man, many other species entered the bloodline. And Shadow might have thought himself human, but the thing is, he was no more human even before Sonya than you are. Rider asked him why no one had made the connection before now. *Your father knew of what he was to you, and worked hard to save you. At great cost to himself. Shadow had no idea who he was to anyone. And he died a man alone. Or so he thought.*

"He was a Lanning. He could have come to us at any time. Family is all we have in the world." Draconal pointed out that he had come to them. "No, I mean before he was so ill that he died. We would have helped him. He should have known he was our family."

And you would have helped him? Even knowing that he was there to kill you? I think not. He did what was necessary to end this without knowing of the connection that you all have. As I said, there were many generations between the first Rider and you.

Rider looked up when Graham came to him. He knew that the guard that had shown up was waiting for him to move away, but he had a connection to the man now. And even though there was nothing left of him, he had been here. The connection was a small one, he supposed, but a connection all the same.

"He did right by us, coming here to save us. And you." Rider held Graham and felt warmed by her love, comforted by her just being with him. "He also told us things, things about our father that seem to make sense. According to my grandparents when they were alive, my father wasn't the man he was with us. He was loving and supportive, as well as a good man to have around when things were bad. Grandma once told me that she thought him to be on drugs, or having a tumor. Even though neither of those would have had any effect on him, I think she wanted to believe that over him just being a bastard."

Things, I have learned over the years, are not always what they appear to be on the surface. Shadow could have easily stayed where he was, doing nothing to save any of us. Or he could have not said a word to you about your father and the things that were done to him. He not only tried to make things right, but he closed the door on a great many questions for you as well. He could simply have left us to die. Because it would have been you and your family's death as well, should he have died with me there. My death would have meant the same for you all in the larger scheme of things. The dragon moved away and Rider pulled Graham into his arms again. But he turned back to speak to him once more before leaving the area altogether. *You will do well as a dragon keeper, young Rider. I look forward to working with you and your family.*

Rider did move back when asked by the head of the royal guard. With Graham beside him, Rider felt better. As soon as the residue was gone that had been left behind by Shadow, he moved to where his family was standing with the others. The grass where Shadow had been was covered in small flowers of the most beautiful shades of purple that Rider had ever seen.

Rider watched too as the shape of the small garden changed. Now it wasn't an outline of the body, but of a dragon. He had to smile when he thought of all the comments that were going to come from this, and was glad that it wasn't his home but Misha's. Kendra and Tristin were sitting on the porch with his family when he and Graham moved to join them.

"They're talking like we're going to be living with them. Kendra and Tristin, I mean. I don't know about that, do you? I mean, we have a home here, family, and my dad has his new building too." He told her that nothing was settled yet. "I guess my dad could come and see us. And we could easily pop in and out of here. It's really almost too easy to do so. And I don't think it would be so bad, would it? Living with dragons in a realm not so different than our own."

"No, not so different, really. I guess if you don't count the unicorns running around, it's normal. I think I saw a few flying creatures, which have long since been thought of as mythical here, on the other realm as well. And they have beautiful weather year around. No rain to speak of that I've ever seen. Oh, and let us not forget that in addition to all that, we have a king and queen as our relatives, a brother who is a prince, as well as a family here that is just as amazing and magical too. Sure, I can see where there is little difference." She smacked him on the chest. "I love you, Graham. And if you think we can take care of a dragon, then I'm with you on that. Hopefully someone will give us some training and we won't get burned if we screw up. That would really suck."

"Yes, a manual would be nice. Here too, on all this crap, but training would help us out a great deal. But I think that, in reality, we really don't have a choice. Do we? I mean, we've been selected to care for the dragons, and now everyone thinks it's a done deal." He shook his head, smiling at her. "So we're dragon trainers now. All right, I can live with that. But I think we should wait a little while, however, before we tell the families. They're much too raw right now to even consider us leaving. I know that I am."

He was as well. So much so, there was so much that had happened in the past few years that had he not lived there with it, he would have been hard pressed to think it all true. But there were good things along with the bad.

They were all mated now, including their mom. Love was abounding in all their homes, and children were coming more and more. They had several new ventures going on as well. Had closed the door on a chapter of their lives that, while stressful, had also brought them great happiness. Rider thought perhaps, just maybe, he might not have to worry so much anymore.

Linyah screamed. It was loud enough to ring in his ears long after she had stopped. No one moved for several seconds until she did it again. Holding her belly, she dropped to her knees and told Thomas she was ready. It took Rider a full minute to realize that she was ready to have their child. As soon as she was carried into the house, worry poured over him like a warm blanket.

He realized then that he was never going to stop worrying about his family.

CHAPTER 12

The dragons were beautiful. And as Graham stood there watching them work the field, she had an overwhelming feeling of completion. Her life, her family's life, felt finished. Not that they were ready to die, but that things were settled down enough now that she knew she could wake in the morning and not have to worry about the next bad guy coming along, or if they were going to be hunted down by some madman.

"My lady?" Graham looked at the woman standing next to her. She had come with the house they were given upon entering the realm here. "There is a matter of your father again, my lady. He is insisting on cooking again."

"No." Marie nodded, her face as grim as Graham was feeling. "Did you explain to him that we have a cook, that there is no reason whatsoever for him to even be in the kitchen?"

"I did, my lady, but he said that you are in need of more protein now, and he wishes to supply you with it. I had to look up what that was, and then I tried to assure him that we were making sure that you and the master of the house had plenty."

Graham nodded but moved to follow Marie to the house as she continued. "The dragons have never been healthier, my lady. And when they feed from you, I don't think your father understands that it is magic they use, not your food supplies."

"Yes, he does. He's just being stubborn. I might have to have him put in irons." Marie stopped so suddenly and turned to look at her that Graham had to laugh. "I was making a joke, Marie. I love my dad very much, and wouldn't put him in the dungeon no matter how many times we have to have the kitchen redone."

Nodding, but still looking unsure, Marie went into the house before her. Graham could smell something cooking. And whatever it was, she was sure it wasn't anything she was going to put to her mouth. It smelled like dragon dung, and she wasn't having any of it.

"Oh, there you are my dear. I was just explaining to my friend here that we need to have more meat in your diet. The dragons will be requiring more and more from you as they continue to breed, so you must be healthy. I've made you something." He offered her his spoon that had been stirring the pot. When she backed from the noxious smell, he looked confused. "It does have a slightly off smell, but I assure you, it's quiet delicious. Or so I've been told."

"You've not tried it?" He told her that he had not. "Okay, so when you've eaten whatever that is, then I'll maybe try it myself."

"I must confess that I cannot get past the smell. But you need to buck up, child, and eat it. It might be the difference between you falling on your face from exhaustion and not." He pushed the spoon toward her again. "Come on now, you want to be strong, don't you?"

"Yes. Right now I'd like to be strong enough to toss you into the yard on your ear and that vile stuff in that pot with you. How about I pour it down your gullet and we'll see how strong you are?" He actually backed away from her. "I see. You know as well as I that it's not going to go anywhere near my mouth, so give it up."

"I'm only trying to be helpful." Her heart melted at his words. "The others don't have a lot of use for a wizard on their realm. Why just yesterday, young Misha asked me to stop giving his daughter teething medications. He claimed that it gave her gaseous emissions enough to have them wearing masks when they change her. I believe him to be over exaggerating that just a little."

"I don't. I was there last week when she dirtied her diaper. The staff wanted to take her to the barn to change her, but they were afraid that the odor would sour the milk of the cow they just got." Her dad said that wasn't possible. "Maybe not, but it was bad, Dad."

"Linyah threatened me as well. Did I tell you that? She said that should I go near her weapons again she will sharpen her knife on my.... Well, it was a very private part of myself, and she looked demented when she saw how I had helped her." Graham asked him what he'd done. "I only wanted to clean them for her. They were all laid out on the table and there were smudges on each of them. How was I to know that my magic would have caused so many problems with them? The magic didn't set well with the knives, and the guns that she used had to be replaced when the casings on them melted. I've never seen such a mess. And when I told her that I'd fix them, I thought she was going to hit me, quite a few times too With the bat she was holding."

Graham had to cover her mouth so he'd not know how funny it was. Linyah had told her that her dad was a delinquent, but she'd never said what he'd done to her. And Thomas had come to her later telling her that her dad needed a hobby. What kind of hobby he had in mind was never discussed, as she'd been called away.

Nildale came to the kitchen just as she was thinking her dad might be acting out because he was lonely. She had thought that he'd come around more often, but he told her that he preferred the other world better, it had more going on. The realm that she now worked and lived in was too perfect. Graham was glad for the realm they lived in, but she could see her dad's point.

"Oh my, this is perfect. Just perfect." Graham asked Nildale what was going on. "I have an issue that I need a wizard or witch for. There seems to be a problem in my gardens. Not the ones around the house, but the orchards as well as the food supply ones. They're not doing as well as we'd hoped."

She started to tell him she'd be glad to help when he winked at her before turning to her dad. As they discussed the things going on in the gardens, the problems that no one seemed to know how to fix, she sat down on the chair and wondered how Nildale had figured it out.

When they left together, their heads close talking about the issues, she looked around the kitchen and saw the staff begin to clean up her dad's mess. With a snap of her fingers the pot and the vile stuff inside was gone, but his herbs and other items would need to be boxed up. A plate of food was set in front of her by Washington, and she smiled up at him.

"It is just a roast beef sandwich with a little mayo as you like it. And momentarily, I shall have you some frenchie fries and catsup." He shook his body as if the mere thought of either of the last things were offensive to him. "Also, my lady, you asked me to remind you of the meeting today."

"Yes. Thank you." She wasn't looking forward to that either.

"Do you know if Linyah and her mom are going to come here first, or am I to meet them there?"

"They are to arrive here at four. And afterwards, I'm to understand that Lady Maribel and the other Lanning ladies will be joining you for tea and cookies. The Lady Queen is holding this in her private chambers." He gave her a plate of the fries and a bottle of her favorite catsup. "Lord Rider has asked that we hold dinner for him tonight. He is joining his brothers for pizza."

Another thing that they'd had to explain to the staff when they'd moved in. It seemed that they had assumed, with the color and all, that catsup was made from cats. She supposed if you really thought about it, it was an odd name. But after showing them the process of making the rich tomato stuff, they were all right with it. But pizza and all the different toppings on it had given them a headache. And when Rider had brought in an all meat one, she thought they were going to quit when he explained sausage to them. Now they just brought what they wanted from the other realm.

After lunch, she went to find Rider. There were a couple of things she needed to get an understanding on, and she wanted to touch him. The man just oozed sexiness, and she wanted to see if he'd be in the mood to take her into the woods before leaving.

When she entered the yard where the dragons were, she watched him from afar while he worked. There was such symmetry about what he was doing, and she thought of a dance when he moved. The dragons were learning to use their bodies in a way to protect the most vulnerable part of them, their bellies, and some of them were doing quite well following his lead.

"Come here and help me." She moved toward him when he spoke. She noticed that he'd taken his shirt off in deference to the heat, and she felt her body respond to his nudity. "You're not helping when you look at me like that."

"I don't care. And if you want to help me, then I'm all for that as well." He growled low and she had to laugh. "You're so wonderfully sexy when you do that. I wonder how no other woman snatched you up before I came along."

"No one else could last a night with my manly skills in bed." She laughed when he did. "Okay, you help me show them what I mean about belly exposure, and I'll take you away from all this and make you scream."

After about ten minutes of play acting that she was trying to stab him, the dragons understood. Rider set two of the older dragons to work watching over them as he took her hand in his. As they set off toward the wooded area behind the fields, all she could think about was how loudly he was going to make her scream.

~~~

Rider had thought of nothing but taking her to the ground since he'd left her in bed this morning. He'd thought that after making love to her all morning it would have been enough. But he found himself wanting her even after he'd drained his body into hers and had brought her several times as well.

"Rider, I need you and your cat." He nearly fell on his face when he stopped to turn and look at her. She was naked. And wet. "Come to me, pretty boy, and lick me."

His cat consumed him. There wasn't any need for him to undress, no reason whatsoever for him to be gentle with her either. Almost as soon as his cat took his body, he was moving toward his mate and licking his lips.

He'd never been gentle with her, and today wasn't going to be any different. As soon as he was close enough to her, the big cat knocked her to the ground and sat between her open thighs.

Rider felt his need for his mate, not just to lick her but to mark her as well. And when he laid his big head on her thigh, he knew that he was going to do so first.

The bite was deep and hard. As soon as Graham screamed, Rider knew that he'd hurt her. But almost before he could beg him to let her go, his cat licked the wounds closed and nudged his head between her wet apex. The first lick had her coming quick.

"More. Make him give me everything." The cat growled low, as if he didn't care for her ordering him about. No sooner had she begged for more than the cat was giving it to her. "Yes, that's it."

He ate at her over and over. Each time he brought her over the edge, his cat would drink her down. Fucking her with his tongue was something that Rider knew that they both enjoyed, and when he brought her a fifth time, Rider asked for his turn. He was between her legs where his cat had been when Graham looked up at him.

"Eat me." He nodded as he slid his fingers deep inside of her. "No, I need your tongue there. Please, I'm so close to coming now that I want to come in your mouth."

"And I wish to watch you while you do." He fucked her with his fingers, his free hand sliding up and down his cock. "When you come like this, I'm going to release all over you, then fuck you. Would you like that?"

Her head nodded as she rode his fingers. Rider loved watching her come. Graham did so with her entire being. And when she screamed out his name, which happened nearly every time, he felt like she had a magical pull on his cock that would make him come harder each time. Christ, he loved this woman.

As she cupped her breasts, pulling and tugging at her nipples, all he could think about was tasting her there, suckling at her breasts like he loved to do. As his balls tightened to his body, his fingers around his shaft going faster, he watched her body bow up, her breasts tighten in anticipation of her release.

"Come for me."

Rider felt his cock release as she screamed. His cum touched her nipples and mouth. When she licked the cream off her with her tongue, he fell forward. Rider took her nipple in his mouth and suckled hard, bringing her again as she held him there. And when she wrapped her legs around his, Rider slammed into her entrance and cried out at the tightness of her sheath, his body ready to come again that quickly.

He fucked her hard, taking her over and over even as he emptied into her three times. As he dropped onto her, rolling at the last minute so as not to hurt her, he held her tightly to him. He loved this woman more every day.

"Rider?" He nodded, unable to speak at that moment. "Rider, would you like to have a child with me?"

He looked at her face, lifting her chin up so that he could see if she was just asking or was really wanting a child. Rider wasn't sure of his answer, but didn't want to say the wrong thing to her if she was kidding.

"A child would be wonderful; don't you think?" She nodded and put her head back down on his chest. "To see you fat with a child would be the best thing I can think of right now. But I'm also willing to wait on that should you want."

"I don't know what I want. A child would be nice, someone we can create together, but our lives, the way we've been running them…seems like years of that would be nice right now." He could agree on that one too. "I'd like to be able to go away like we did after agreeing to come here. I enjoyed seeing Paris with you, as well as the falls in New York. I'm not sure that we could do that with a baby, are you?"

"We have time to think on that." When she nodded, he said nothing more. Just thinking about her having his child was making his cat stir, as if telling him that he was ready for a playmate as well.

Linyah had had her baby a little over three months ago. Then just last month Murph had gone into labor and had her baby. There were so many small ones around the houses now that Rider found himself spending time in the yard. It wasn't that he disliked children, he loved all his nieces and nephews, but he found himself worrying about the slightest little thing about them.

Last week when they'd been home, Misha had laughed at him for a good hour when his son had sneezed out this slimy green goop that had made Rider slightly nauseous. The baby had acted like it wasn't that big of a deal that this long stream of stuff was hanging on his lip, and when he licked it into his mouth, Rider had to give the kid to his mom and leave the room. Kids were gross.

As he held onto Graham thinking about nothing in particular, Misha contacted him. His brother had been doing that a lot lately, just contacting him with nothing more than to tell him hi. Today, it seemed that he had a question.

I'm wondering about something that Walker just asked me. You know the deal better than most of us. When we gave him the contract, did we mention the option for him to make us partners? Before Rider could answer him, Misha was talking again. *I've tried and tried to get him to just take the property. He's our stepfather now, but he insists that its bad business to do that. What business? He's our family.*

I think that he might be right about the partnership deal. It's in the contract with him. Something like if the business does well, I don't remember the numbers now, but if it does well enough, we can form a partnership if all parties agree. But he did agree with Misha, the man should have the property for making their mom so happy if nothing else. *You might just want to have a paper drawn up and hand it all over to Mom. I'm betting she'll make him see reason.*

You'd think that, wouldn't you? But you know what she did? She threatened me. Told me if I tried to do something underhanded she'd make me regret it. And I don't know about you, but I'm still afraid of Mom when she gets all riled up like this. Rider told him she didn't even have to be riled up for him to be afraid. *I love her to death, but she has one hell of a temper.*

They talked about how to handle the partnership and what to do about the land. Rider said he could go and talk to the banker when he was home next, and Misha told him thanks. Then he asked when he was coming home again.

Two weeks for Max's graduation from college. I can't believe that kid is well on his way to getting his doctorate right now. Misha said he couldn't either. *What did you get him for graduation?*

Believe it or not, I've no idea what to get him. What did you end up getting? Rider told him. *Hey, I like that. A building. That's pretty good. I might have to think of something along those lines too. He'll need an office, right? Perhaps I can get something in the downtown area for him to start working on now. Yes, I love that. Thanks.*

No problem. But so you know, the one that Graham and I got for him is a former bank. I think he might have fun with that. The safe is still inside as well. I was talking to Nildale and Sina about it, and they're going to do some remodeling of it for him. Make the place a home for him to use when he's older. Misha laughed and said that he thought Max had been born old. *Yeah, there is that.*

When Graham looked up at him, he could see that she'd been asleep while lying there. Telling her that he'd been talking to Misha, she got up and dressed. Rider was both disappointed and relieved. She'd worn him out again. Closing down the connection between himself and Misha, he sat up and dressed himself. Rider asked her if everything was all right.

"Yes. Why do you ask?" He shrugged and told her she looked pensive. "Pensive? Do people even say that anymore? Okay, I am a little pensive, but for the life of me, I have no idea why. We have everything going right for the moment. And I'm happier than I've ever been. We have a nice place to live, plenty of money, and work. Nothing is chasing us and we don't have to go out and kill things. What is wrong with me?"

"I was thinking we need to go shopping again." She started to shake her head. "The Route Forty thing starts in two weeks."

The glimmer in her eyes told him that it was perfect. They'd had so much fun going there and shopping for the stores. They had a team doing it now, people from the pack going to auctions and garage sales finding things. But they'd found each other, so to speak, and he wanted to do it again. With her.

"Last time we did that, we saw a lot of people in motor homes with trailers. We don't need a trailer, not with our magic, but I would love to have a camper to stay in." He nodded, warming to the idea. "Not one of those little ones, but I don't want a house on wheels either."

"We could actually have one of the little ones and expand the inside the way we need it. Sort of like you did with your home with Allister." She nodded and he could see that she was getting into this idea. "And we'd not have to pack much in the way of clothing and other items either."

"No. We have everything we need now. How long would we be gone?" He told her they could do the whole trail this time. "Yes. And anything we get, we can have it taken there easily enough while we're still out. We'd have to make arrangements with Laci and the dragons."

"I've already spoken to Draconal. He thinks it's a splendid idea. And he has agreed to watch over things for us while we're gone. I might have to pop back in for something, but that shouldn't be too bad." Graham leaped into his arms and he held her to him. "I'm assuming you like this idea of mine."

"You know that I do. I love you for this. I loved it when we did it last year, and was actually thinking about a way to convince you to go again." He laughed when she kissed him all over his face. "You're the best man in the world. Taking his poor wife on a road trip with a camper to pick up dusty old things. Thank you."

He kissed her again, glad now that he'd had a reminder email sent to him last year. Rider decided not to tell her that he'd been worried about convincing her to go. They were going to have so much fun.

CHAPTER 13

Max looked around the room. There wasn't much going on at the moment. Everyone was waiting on news from the doctor and resting up for the big event. It had been a very long night for them all. Leaning back against the wall and closing his eyes, he smiled when someone leaned their head against his shoulder.

"Babies take so long." He told his sister that they took the amount of time that they needed. "That's a stupid answer and you know it. It's like the other day when you told me that the day isn't long, it's the same as the one before it. And it'll be the same as the next day. You know as well as I do that I meant it felt long."

"But it was the truth." He looked at his little sister. "You're supposed to be reading that book for school. Have you?"

"Yes. Twice, like you told me. It was better the second time." Leila, named for their grandmother, smiled up at him. "You should have been a teacher, Maxie. The girls would all have been in love with you, and I would have been the most popular girl around."

"I like what I do. And you are the most popular girl around. The kids all love you." Max tickled her as he continued. "Stop calling me Maxie. I'm Doctor Maxie to you, young lady, and you know it."

When she laughed with him, he put his arm around her shoulders and held her. Leila was the best sister a guy could ask for. She was smart and brave. Happy and full of life. He found himself at times seeking her out so he could have some of her happiness. Not that he wasn't happy, but his job drained him all the time.

Max had become a surgeon just as he wanted to do all along. And according to his last internal review, was the best at what he did. Of course he had an advantage over most doctors. He had a great deal of magic that aided him not only in what he did, but what he was able to find once he opened someone up. Max had saved countless lives in his short tenure as a surgeon, and would save many more. Not that he'd not lost a few along the way, but he did save as many as he could.

He looked at Leila when she sighed heavily. "Have you told Mom and Dad what you want to be? I know that you've started taking some online classes toward that goal. Don't take on too much. You'll miss out on things if you think you have to study all the time." When she shook her head, he told her why they needed to know. "They can open doors for you that you won't be able to at your age. And so can the family. Mom has helped me so much getting into some college classes that I wouldn't have been able to take as young as I was."

"I talked to Grandma Maribel about it, and she and Grandpa Walker are going to help me. Grandpa Walker is going to hire me as an intern this summer so I can get my feet wet. It won't be much, but it'll be something." He nodded, knowing about the job that had been created just for Leila and the kind of work she'd be doing. But learning to file played a part in her education too. "His warehouse is expanding again. Did you hear?" He had and was very proud of his family.

When Grandpa Walker had come to town with the plan to open a warehouse in their town, he had not only found that he could make it work here but that he'd find the love of his life. Grandma Maribel was so happy now, what with babies coming all the time and a mate that loved her like she deserved, Max found himself hanging out at their house a great deal. He had even taken to having dinner with the family now when his schedule permitted it.

One of the hardest things he'd had to learn was that he had to do this on his own. He could have depended on his family to bail him out all the time and they would have gladly done it for him. But Max knew that if he was going to learn anything from the school of hard knocks, as Uncle Misha called it, he was going to have to learn to fall on his ass and get up on his own.

"Grandpa Walker asked me to come oversee his onsite clinic the other day. It's a nice one. About as up to date as most hospitals now. And they've expanded their employee base too. From just over six hundred to nearly a thousand. I think he has plans to build a manufacturing plant here as well." He looked up when a nurse came toward them. When she passed them by with a wink to him, he continued talking to Leila. "What did you get for the new baby?"

He still had a hard time when someone flirted with him. And it happened a great deal. Once, when he'd been talking to a patient at the hospital, he'd had to call security to have them take the daughter of the woman away. She'd not only come on to him, but had stripped down naked and had begged him to beat her with the whip she'd brought. He'd been worried to death every day since that someone would lock him in a room and tie him up. Changing the subject, he looked at Leila.

"Books. Both fictional and true to life. I thought to broaden their pallet." He had to laugh. It was what she got all the babies when they came into the world. And even at only being nine years old, she had given a lot of baby books. "What did you get for him?"

"Magic." She nodded, knowing that whatever the babies weren't born with, he'd give them what he could. Max wanted his family safe. He knew better than most what sort of monsters were out there. And not just paranormals either. Some humans were about as bad as they could be. For one so young, Max thought he'd seen a lot more than most.

Max was now nearly twenty-one years old. He had two sisters, one of them Leila and the other, now five, named Sarah. As well as a little brother due in a month. The little boy—Andrew, they were going to call him—was going to be strong like him, and just as smart. Max hadn't told his parents yet, but he would soon. Andrew, named for his grandfather that had been killed, was going to need a great deal of training. His magic was going to be strong.

His mom and dad had also taken in several children to raise. They had, of course, asked him if it was all right, as if he'd tell them no. But they'd saved a lot of children in their own right. Taking them in when tragedy had taken one or both of their parents from them. Several of them had come to his parents in the middle of the night because their own parents were too drugged up or in jail. Max had helped as much as he could, but his mom said that they needed to do this. Much like Uncle Rider and Aunt Graham did antique shopping. It was just what they needed to feel better about life.

The children, ranging from nearly his age now to four, were well cared for, fed, and clothed. Given a good education when they wanted it and jobs at the distribution center when they were ready for one. His mom and dad were the best parents there could be in the world, and he loved every single one of the kids they brought into his life.

Max looked over at Misha and Hannah. They had only the one child of their own, but had opened their doors to many more, just as his parents had. In the ten years since he'd joined the family with his mom, his aunt and uncle had taken in not just children into their home, but a few adults too that needed a helping hand.

Several times in the last few years his family had helped a few families get their feet back under them when they'd lost everything due to circumstances beyond their control. Some of it due to loss of income, others due to a death. A few times because of illness that made it impossible for one or both of the parents to work. They were given comfort, support, and the means to get going again. Several buildings in town had been set up for transient circumstances; places to stay until deposits could be saved up or money for a much needed car was found.

Max thought that the children of these families, even the adults, still called Hannah up just to talk. But one thing she would not condone or help with was abuse. The first time a hand was raised against another she would toss them out on the sidewalk, and then run them out of town on her own. Hannah had a way about her that would make someone think she was a major pushover. And she was until you pissed her off. Then you'd better have your life in order, because she was gunning for you. Max loved her for it too.

His Uncle Thomas had been spending a lot of time in the

other realm lately with Aunt Linyah. Aunt Kendra and Uncle Tristin were having their fourth child soon, and his aunt and uncle were helping them out with the kingdom. Max knew that Uncle Thomas didn't much care for the duties as a whole, but he loved them and would do anything in the world for anyone.

Max knew that his Grandma Sina and Grandpa Nildale were having a wonderful holiday right now. They were touring countries at will, visiting chapels and churches, as well as trying new foods. So far Max had heard that they'd enjoyed sushi, but had not liked much in the way of foods with cabbage in them. Grandpa Nildale had claimed it wasn't fit to eat. Grandma had told him it wasn't too bad, but she'd not eat it again. Just yesterday they were in Ireland visiting a ruined castle. He'd gotten an email this morning with pictures of them having a fine meal in a pub. They were wonderful people too.

Max knew that they weren't his real grandparents; most of the extended family that he had wasn't related to him at all by blood. But he loved them no less than if they were his own real family. Grandma Leila had told him you only get one chance at family, and he'd better not screw it up. Max had been working hard his whole life to not just keep them safe, but to not screw up. He thought so far he'd done a good job.

He glanced at her now, his Grandma Leila. She was sitting in the chair with her dog at her feet, one she'd chosen after the death of Roger, the one he'd given her so long ago. This dog was as much loved by his grandma as his grandfather had been. Ranger was just as loving too. It had nearly devastated her when Roger had passed away a few years ago. Max thought perhaps Grandma Leila had taken precautions with this new friend of hers and given him long life. The two of them were inseparable now, and he thought perhaps she might have forgiven him now for giving her the first pup. He had peed on a lot of carpets before she'd had a long talk with him. Grandma Leila expected perfection, even in her doggy companions.

Uncle Andrew and Aunt Laci had five children. Triplet girls born on his birthday, and twin boys born three years ago. They were often found in the backyard of their home rather than in it, playing and having fun with the kids. Uncle Andrew and her still went to auctions to buy antiques for their shop, but now took the kids with them. They had nine antique stores now, all over the United States. And Max thought they were having the time of their life cleaning up the things they got cheap and sold for a profit. Even the kids were getting pretty good at it, he thought.

Aunt Charlie wasn't here yet; her shop had gotten busy at the last minute, but she was coming, she told them. Uncle Phillip was sitting with Misha, holding one of his boys on his lap to save him from some tragedy as they talked. Aunt Charlie had given birth to a wonderful set of twin boys that were eight now, and a little girl who was the same age as his youngest sister. Their store, both online and a physical one, had done so well that they'd expanded to several other towns in states all over. Aunt Charlie still had a hard time being in the public eye at times, but with Uncle Phillip helping her, she did well. The kids were a great distraction for her when she needed them to be. Max was really proud of them all.

His mom consulted with the FBI now. It had been a shock to him when she'd said that she was helping out. Not that she couldn't do it, but he knew that she had been so happy when Lanning Rescue had closed down. She told him later that she'd been burnt out. But this job, just consulting and not actually going on the missions, was much better. Dad would oftentimes hold down the fort when she had to travel. Or they'd make a nice trip of it if there was time for him to make arrangements at his own store. Bits and Pieces was doing well too, as he'd known it would. Having a centralized place for people to find the perfect doorknob or even a hinge had been a big hit. And he was pretty sure that they had fun at it too, finding things and taking them apart for resale. Max thought he had the best of both worlds with his mom and dad. A ready-made family, as well as brothers and sisters a lot like he was. Doran.

Uncle Rider was coming down the hall then. Max stood up and reached out to see if things were all right. He had made a promise to them when they told them that they were expecting not to let anyone know the sex of the baby, nor anything else he might have found out. He was relieved to find everyone was well and happy. Max was grinning when everyone stood up too and started asking him questions. The first one was, is Graham all right?

"Yes, she's wonderful. But, I know you guys have been hounding us to death on the baby. I'm happy to say that Graham is doing well, tired but well, and that we're parents." Max laughed when Misha asked him what the baby was. "Two little girls. And two little boys."

No one moved. Grandma Maribel looked the most shocked, and had to be helped to a chair by Grandpa Walker. When she asked him if he was kidding, Uncle Rider shook his head.

"You had four? Four babies?" He nodded, and Max thought he was going to hurt himself by smiling so much. "Oh my, Rider. You have a family of ten now."

"Yes. This is all for us for a while, too." Uncle Rider looked around the room as he continued. "I'm the most blessed man in the world. Not only do I have the best family in the entire world, both of them as a matter of fact, but I have eight of the most wonderful children, a wife that loves me for some reason, and a job that every kid in the world wishes they had. I get to work with dragons and unicorns."

It was nearly an hour before they could go back and see the new momma. Max had known, of course, that they were having quadruplets, had even known that they were boys and girls. But what no one knew but him was that these babies were special. The dragon, Draconal, had made sure of it. These were going to be the next generation of dragon keepers.

Uncle Rider had taken the job as keeper tentatively. He'd not wanted to take a job over and be bored, was what he'd told his Grandma Sina. Max was pretty sure that he'd never been bored since he'd taken over, and had, in his grandma's words, made everyone happy when he had agreed to it. Including Draconal, the king of dragons. Uncle Rider had been, quite literally, born to the job. He and Aunt Graham had done a wonderful job of it too.

They did live on the other realm, that was true. But since everyone was able to go back and forth between the two worlds, it wasn't like he was gone from them for good. Most of the time they'd make it back here to have dinner, or come to planned events. But there were times when it wasn't possible.

Max had helped them a couple of times when there was a difficult birth. Not of the dragons as they hatched, but when the other creatures would come into the world. Max had helped bring not just a few unicorns into the world, but several trolls, a centaur, and even a Pegasus or two. He wondered briefly what his colleagues would think if he told them that he'd not just seen a few flying horses, but had had the pleasure of bringing them into the world as well. He was pretty sure that they'd think him nuts.

When they were finally taken to see the babies, Max touched

his fingers to each of their cheeks, feeling the magic that had been given to them through the big dragon. He added his own little bit to them, knowing that they'd be stronger even than their parents when they grew up. Max was glad every day that he'd been taken under the care of the Lanning Leap.

~~~

Rider felt amazing. His children were here, all eight of them with the older ones now, and they were all healthy. As he held the newest additions to his growing family, he looked at his son, Patrick, his oldest at six years. And named for the first Rider that had been born. Rider was a little nervous that he was going to be like him, someone to worry too much and to be organized to the point of annoyance. But he loved him with all his heart.

"Do you suppose they're going to be a mess like Delilah is?" Rider assured him that as there were four of them, they'd be messier. "Great. I guess I'm going to have to make a bigger chart for them."

"Chart?" Patrick nodded as he studied the little girl in his arms. "What sort of chart do you have to make bigger? Do you mean the one that Mommy made so you got your summer reading done?"

"I did all the reading for that chart. She's letting me read some of the books in your library. No, I was talking about the chart that I fixed up for cleaning up after each other. Davey and Delilah would just let all their toys lay all over their room and someone might trip over them. So I made them a chart that tells them when they have to pick up." Patrick looked up at him. "I was afraid that you'd go into their room at night and fall over something, and I'd not be there to help you up."

"Patrick, you do realize that the one time I fell over it wasn't because of toys, right? I got hit in the chest by a wing, and it only knocked the wind out of me, it didn't hurt me." He nodded, looking at the bassinet that held his other sister and brothers. "They're going to be just fine, and so will I."

"I know, Daddy, but I still worry." Rider loved being called that; Daddy was a wonderful title. "Uncle Misha said I'm the pitting image of you."

"It's spitting, not pitting, and you are. And that scares me more than you know." He asked him why. "Never mind. Just try and relax a little. You're only six."

"Almost seven." Rider didn't point out that he'd only been six for a month and he wasn't almost seven. His son, was a great deal like him, and Rider wasn't sure whether he should be proud or scared.

After his brothers took the other children home with them to spend the night, Rider lay on the bed with Graham and held her to his body. He loved this woman, more than he'd ever thought was possible.

"I'm supposed to tell you to make sure that when the doctor comes in to check on me, that you're holding on to something so you don't fall again." He asked Graham if it was Patrick that had told her to do that. "Yes. He has it in his head that you're a clumsy dork."

"He did not call me a dork." She laughed and he hugged her tighter. "My mom is about to bust with all these children now. She told me that she now has to go and rethink her gifts. I told her that we weren't going to dress them the same so she'd be fine. I don't think she liked my answer."

"No, she told me that she had to go out and buy another of each outfit. I wonder if she realizes that they have so many hand me downs now that it's doubtful that they'd have to wear the same outfit twice before they outgrew it." Rider said that she

187

more than likely didn't care. "No, she'd only want to shower them with gifts like she does the other grandchildren."

Rider knew when Graham had fallen asleep. He could feel her even breaths as she rested, her heartbeat under his hand as he held her. When he was sure that she'd not wake when he got up, he made his way to the bassinet where his children were.

"Hello, little people." They, too, were asleep but for James, the youngest boy. Picking him up now, he walked to the rocker that had been put in the room with them and sat holding him. "You're very handsome, has anyone ever told you that before?"

The baby yawned but continued to stare at him. Rider rocked a little, and wondered, not for the first time since becoming a father, how he'd come to be so lucky. And so loved.

"We've had an addition put on the house for you guys. I think you'll like it. I know that I do. Your mommy also decided that she wanted help this time too, after you're all home. I will, of course, do whatever she wants because your mom has given me so much, but with eight children in the house, we're going to be a little spread out. You guys are just perfect." He rocked a little more, noticing the mark on his son, and lifted his small hand up to look at it closer. When he put it back on his little chest, Rider had to close his eyes when he thought of what it meant.

James had the mark of the dragon. It was a beautiful one too. Bright purple like the dragon he was sure had given it to him. Rider knew that he was looking at his future replacement, and he couldn't have been more proud and terrified at the same time. Rider started rocking again when James fussed a little.

"I should tell you now that I'm not sure what to think about this. Your mark, like mine, means that you're going to watch over the dragons. They're a sight, let me tell you." He thought of his first time seeing them. "I had it in my head that there was only a few. Draconal, the oldest dragon ever born, as well as a couple of others. There were over two thousand of them when I went to their compound. Two thousand of the most beautiful winged creatures that I have ever seen. And someday, you will be their keeper. Just as I am now. What do you think of that?"

Rocking more, trying his best to get a handle on the mark and what all came with it, he started to get up and see if the other three had it too. But the longer he sat there, the more he realized that looking now or later wouldn't change a thing, so he decided he'd look later, when he was less overwhelmed by it.

"I love you, son." He looked at his little boy and saw the startling purple eyes that both his mother and the dragon had. "You're going to be the best dragon keeper there has ever been. You and your brother and sisters, you're going to do a much better job than I could ever hope to have done. I love you all so very much."

Rider rocked him until James finally fell asleep in his arms. He didn't get up to put him to bed, but continued to hold him, needing these extra moments with his child more than he'd realized. Loving a child wasn't hard; it was giving them up to the world that was the most difficult.

Rider had a lot going on in his head right now, more than he could nail down at any given moment, but he did think that whatever happened, he was going to just roll with it. The laughter from the corner of the room had him looking over at Nildale.

"You no more believe that than I do. Rider Lanning does not just let things roll. At least not the Rider I know." Rider only grinned at the man. "I have come to see them. I thought you'd be resting with that young bride of yours."

"I was for a time, but I thought she'd rest better if I wasn't there. The bed is much smaller than the one we have at home."

Looking over at his love, he wasn't really surprised to see the bed was larger, the blankets on them the same as the ones that they had at home. The entire room, even the pictures on the walls, were as if they were nowhere but their home. "Thank you. It'll be much homier for us this way."

"It's my pleasure. No one else will see it as such. And if they need to be getting into closets, you'll see it the old way momentarily, but it's what you both need." Rider nodded his thanks again. "Now then. Let me see these babes of yours. Four babies, Rider. How did one man have such luck?"

Nildale took Kelsey, the oldest girl, from the bassinet. She fussed for a moment, but as soon as Nildale settled in his own rocking chair, she quieted down. Rider, for the moment, was content just to sit there with his dear friend. Nildale too, it seemed, wasn't ready to speak. Then the king lifted up her hand and Rider could see that she was marked as well.

"They're all marked, I think. Were you aware that was going to happen to them? I don't mind, but it would have been nice to have known." Nildale said that he'd not known that all of them would be, but was glad for it. "Me too, I guess. I mean, with the dragon families growing more and more monthly, the extra hands will be nice. Did you have anything to do with them being chosen like this?"

"Nay, I did not. But I, as I said, knew that at least one of them would be marked. It's the way it should be. I've been doing some reading on it, books in our own realm, and it says that when a keeper has children, there are some for him and some for the dragons. Perhaps this means you're going to have more children?" They both laughed. Right now, Rider was happy the way they were. "Kendra told me a few weeks ago that she had been surprised that all of them hadn't been marked, but she said you and they were young yet. Mayhap they're going to come into their marks. It's happened before." Rider didn't feel young at the moment, but said nothing. Nildale looked down at the bundle in his arms. "Draconal sends his love and good wishes. I'm assuming you know that you'll need to bring them to him when you can. Now that we know who they are, he'll have to smell them. I've never seen such a happy dragon as he is."

"He told me that I should name one for him someday." Nildale looked up at him, smiling. "You know I did it. Graham insisted. I think she loves the old dragon as much as she does me. Perhaps at times more so. He'll do things for her that I cannot get him to do. Such as rest more. He's getting up there in years."

"He is, that he is. Draconal was made, I know you're aware of that. So he didn't grow to be as he is, but was always fully what he is now. And I don't know who might have created him, such a wonderful creature. But once he was with us, other dragons came to be there as well. His own mate, I think, was created by him. So? You've named one for him, have you? What is it? And I won't tell him. Which child is his?" Rider thought that a strange thing to say, but answered him anyway. "Oh, what a lovely name. He'll be so pleased. You couldn't have done better with it. We will need to celebrate once you're home and rested. Yes, a large welcoming party will be just the thing."

Rider and Nildale spoke for a little while longer. He told him of his plans to enlarge the grounds that the dragons worked in. Nildale mentioned to him about the newest members of court that had been inducted a few days ago. They often sat like this, without the babies of course, just talking about their day. Rider had come to look forward to the visits from the man; he thought of him as a kind of father. And of course, he'd be a grandfather to these children as he was to the others.

191

"When I was first told of you and the other Lanning men, I came to see for myself how your family had fared over the centuries. I was there the day that you were hurt and Misha shot. I couldn't intervene much, of course, but I was there. I knew, you see, even then that you'd be a part of our lives. Not how, but I knew it." Rider asked him how much he had helped them. "I shouldn't say. You worry enough as it is. But Misha never made it. Neither of you did. The man, the madman, he murdered first your brother then you. Your dear mother, she passed as well, the pain of it too much for her to bear. The rest of you, as you're aware now, they didn't survive either by Sonya's hand. As you know, you and Misha, you're the backbone and the muscle to this family. Even before we came into your lives."

It was a lot to take in. If not for the help of one person, this man in front of him, his entire family would have been wiped out. Not only by an insane woman, but a man as well. He looked down at the son in his arms, a child that he created with the love of a great woman, and held him tighter to him. No one that now joined their family would have been here if Nildale had not come to check on his family.

"I owe you more than I can ever begin to repay." Nildale told him it had been his pleasure. "Maybe so, but you saved the lives of everyone in my house, my family, and any extended families too. When I think of what would have happened.... Max and Murph would be dead. All our spouses would have died as well, because we weren't there to help them. There would be no children. My mom wouldn't have found her second chance at love. I would never have met my Graham and had these wonderful additions to my life. I love you, Nildale. And if you'd allow it, I'd be honored if you'd allow me to call you Dad. You've been one to me more than my own, and I need you in my life."

"I love you as well, Rider. More than I thought possible. And yes, it would honor me should you call me Dad." Nildale stood up then and came to him. As he held out his hand to him, Rider didn't hesitate to take it. The power coming through the touch wasn't magical, as had happened in the past, but it was the power of love. "You're the best of the best."

After he left them, leaving the chair as a gift for the youngest Lanning children, Rider put James to bed and crawled into bed with his wife. There was room now for them, but he still moved as close as he could get without waking her. He was excited about taking them home, and nervous as well.

Just before he fell asleep, Draconal reached out to him.

Congratulations, my son. I hear everything went well. He told him it had and that everyone was doing fine. *You'll need them, I think. To help with all that is going on here. Well, tell me their names. I wish to send them a little token of my appreciation for taking over my care one day.*

You did this. Draconal pretended to not know what Rider was talking about, but he knew. *You marked my children. You needed all four? Whatever will they do but trip all over each other? Now I'm thinking that I'll have to rethink the name of one of my children. I don't care for being tricked.*

Draconal laughed, his humor filling Rider with such warmth. *We are growing, my son. Soon there will be too many for you to even care for.* Rider knew that as well. Just recently six new hatchlings were born. *I would have liked to have been there, but I think, under the circumstances, it was best I stayed here. Now. Tell me their names.*

James Darin and Jessie Ellison are the boys, and one of my daughters is named Kelsey Dawn. Draconal told him they were sound names. Good strong ones. Then he asked after the last child. *Her name is Maribel Draconal Lanning.*

A finer name than I've ever heard. Your mother, she'll be as pleased as me, I think. A child named for me deserves such wonders, don't you think? Rider told him that he didn't have to do anything special for her. They'd named her for him because they liked him very much. *Even so, you named a girl child for me. I'll have to think of something special for her. Mayhap I'll create her a dragon mate. One that can shift such as yourself. A man of worth, to carry on the name of my namesake. What think you, Rider of the dragons? A dragon mate for your daughter?*

I think that should such a man come to my child, I might hurt you both. I don't even want to think of my little girl having a mate and all that might go with that. They both laughed. *But the thought of her having a child of your own creation coming to her, it makes me feel wonderful. I cannot think of a better way for the continuation of both our lines.*

Then I shall gather my magic around me. I will need to think of the perfect man for her. One that we can both be proud of and love. Rider said he'd like that. *Rider of the dragons, you have humbled me.*

After closing the connection between them, Rider wrapped his body around Graham. He was nearly asleep when he thought of how he was going to manage a houseful of children. Smiling, he realized that they'd do it, simply because they were Lannings. And Lannings were very good at adapting to any situation. Or so he hoped.

LANNING'S LEAP SERIES

Before You Go...

HELP AN AUTHOR

write a review

THANK YOU!

Share your voice and help guide other readers to these wonderful books. Even if it's only a line or two your reviews help readers discover the author's books so they can continue creating stories that you'll love. Login to your favorite retailer and leave a review. Thank you.

AWARD WINNING, BESTSELLING AUTHOR

Kathi Barton, author of the bestselling series Force of Nature, lives in Nashport, Ohio with her husband Paul. In addition to writing full time Kathi likes to spend time with her eight grandkids, three children and three children-in-laws. She writes to relax and have fun.

Her muse, a cross between Jimmy Stewart and Hugh Jackman, brings them to life for her readers in a way that has them coming back time and again for more. Her favorite genre is paranormal romance with a great deal of spice. You can visit Kathi online and drop her an email if you'd like. She loves hearing from her fans. aaronskiss@gmail.com.

Follow Kathi on her blog: http://kathisbartonauthor.blogspot.com/

www.ingramcontent.com/pod-product-compliance
Lightning Source LLC
Chambersburg PA
CBHW032134170626
46808CB00006B/2229